LOVE & the bottle

LOVE & the bottle

Don Kerr

Edited by Bonnie Burnard.

Cover photo by Mad Cow Studio, Regina, Saskatchewan.

Cover and book design by Duncan Campbell.

Printed and bound in Canada at Houghton-Boston Lithographers, Saskatoon, Saskatchewan.

Canadian Cataloguing in Publication Data

Kerr, Don.
Love & the bottle
ISBN 1-55050-161-5

I. Title. II. Title: Love and the bottle.

PS88571.E71 L68 2000 C813'.54 C00-920036-3
PR9199.3.K4264 L68 2000

COTEAU BOOKS
401-2206 Dewdney Ave.
Regina, Saskatchewan
Canada S4R 1H3

AVAILABLE IN THE US FROM
General Distribution Services
4500 Witmer Industrial Estates
Niagara Falls, NY, 14305-1386

The publisher gratefully acknowledges the financial assistance of the Saskatchewan Arts Board, the Canada Council for the Arts, the Government of Canada through the Book Publishing Industry Development Program (BPIDP), and the City of Regina Arts Commission, for its publishing program.

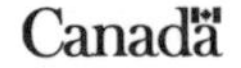

To all the good editors

contents

Baby Duck

I knew I was in trouble again when I forgot how to get off the bus. She was sitting one seat back of the exit paying no attention to anyone – looking straight ahead like she couldn't see anything. Blonde with a yellow bandana and huge eyes.

I kept reading over the top of my paperback at her. Bus turns the corner and I go to get off only I'm looking at her, close-up. She's wearing a blouse the colour of lilacs and quite loose and cool and tight jeans and I just stand there and forget to push the bar on the door.

> You gettin off or not? It's the bus driver. Push the bar.

I don't say anything, though that second or two is a long one and gets longer when I think about it later. I'm outside feeling like a fool but a lot of people didn't turn around so only the driver and I and a guy at the back know what a fool I am. And her, maybe her.

I walk down the street under the trees so it's part

shade part sun and suddenly I see the houses as if I hadn't seen them before. It's afternoon and they all look asleep. Hot summer eyelids closed, nobody looking out so I'm just what I want to be, anonymous. I imagine love going on in all the hot shady bedrooms, or kitchens, or...better get some milk, and I go into the confectionery and even the proprietor, mother of how many I don't even know, looks good in this heat so I know I'm in real trouble. I buy tonic water too, got to drink this heat away.

Get home and find the bloody kids have drunk the gin so it's back to the bus but I'm a veteran now and there's no lilac going downtown to the government liquor supermarket where it's air-conditioned and has a shady kind of light. It's like going to a lake in the centre of town. Get my London Dry after a bit of window shopping and there she is again, just like a French movie our paths crossing. She's looking at the tequila section like it's a foreign country.

I could offer her some advice.

I'm as good at liquor as I'm bad at women. She puts the Sauza back on the shelf, gets a six pack of Boh. I'm behind her in the lineup concentrating on her behind. She says, Oh, turns around, has forgotten something, sees me.

You're the guy that couldn't get off the bus.

Bus? I reply, as if it were as foreign as tequila.

I'm next in line so I pay, booze put in an anonymous brown bag so nobody knows I'm a drinker and I watch her go down the Canadian wine section and come back with Baby Duck.

Jesus. Could you love a woman who drinks Baby Duck?

Next it'll be Lonesome Charlie, Spumante Bambino, Muskrat Ramble, Beaver Dam. Cripes. Wait a minute. Maybe she's buying it for her baby brother. Maybe she's got a boyfriend – she's got to have a boyfriend – and he drinks it. Dumb bastard.

She pays. Cashier never even giggles. They're hardened to people buying soap opera booze.

I open the automatic door for her.

Baby Duck eh?

Oh it's you.

Like to go for a drink?

Piss off you stupid shit.

That's Baby Duck talk. She's going to fill that body with that booze.

Sorry, miss, I say.

I am taller so I can speak taller like a person who drinks scotch and soda or gin and tonic. And off she goes, speaking better with her ass than her mouth.

Later that night I'm still thinking of the blouse, sitting in the backyard to keep cool with a who's-counting gin and tonic. Gin. The perfume of alcohols. So who's to talk, nobody's perfect. But I've an elegant tongue and I begin to imagine dialogues between the blouse and myself, and the jeans and myself, but I won't write that one down. I'd be a bit ashamed to see it in daylight.

I should think about something else. Maybe tomorrow I'll watch for a woman who buys Cuervo Gold.

Tiger Lily

I'll tell you how far I've gone for her. I've entered the marathon. It's a short marathon I admit, about three miles, but I've only ever run for things like the bus, one block at most, or to first base, but I was always a weak hitter.

I entered to win an argument with her. She can drive you crazy because, and I am a history teacher so I like point form, she is 1) not that beautiful but beautiful enough; 2) I know she wears a brassiere which helps the shape but I can't help leaning towards it; 3) she can cook and she can laugh; but 4) she keeps telling me what I ought to do with my life and in particular that 5) I only think of myself. Arguing with her is more difficult than establishing the causes for World War I. She has said once a week for eight years I only think of myself, and when I'm away she'll write that.

So now I'm in the marathon. And not for myself. I hate to run. I even hate watching other people run. It's for some group, the dispeptics I think. I'll make them some money. And prove that I can act for other people and not for myself. I can be absolutely selfless. And win an argument too.

Race begins at the football stadium, goes along the river, down the road allowance and back through the ritzy Lakeside subdivision. There's hundreds of us at the starting line. Guys having a last smoke. Girls touching their toes. I haven't done that for about eighteen years but it's not that great an experience. Guy next to me who's got a number on his jersey says I shouldn't race in hush puppies.

That's okay, they're old ones.

No, I mean you can hurt your feet when you run.

It's okay, I say, I don't want to win.

In fact losing is best. No sense of self at all. I don't run to win. I run so all the dispeptics can win, or the single fathers or whatever. Affirmative action for lung disease. Research into shin splints. Let's hear it for a retirement home for old joggers. Get them off the street. I've had to close the blinds and drink there's so many of them.

Okay, it's your funeral.

It's that guy next to me still talking. Funeral. Maybe that'll impress her. Dying blood-shod at the finish line.

Gun goes off and we're away, hundreds of us. I'm stuck in the middle and I actually have to run for a while. It even feels good. But I fall back, with a good deal of class I think, like a guy waltzing off the dance floor when they put on the rock and roll. I become last with a certain amount of style. Dead last. The race is going according to plan.

I get to the river doing little better than a walk and come to the first suck-a-lemon stand, which is already closing up and the lady looks at me like I've just come for the free lemons. She looks like she sucks lemons or has been married for a long time. I start up running again, over top of the river. Sensible river too, going to the sea at a walking pace. I do a little real run, get a stitch in my side and walk. It is beautiful out here, quiet now the marathon's gone ahead, a prairie day with great parades of clouds so it's like being in the tall cool mountains too. Never been on the riverbank here before. God won't know where I'm at. He'd never look for me running. I should never be here on a Saturday afternoon. I'm free, I think, I'm free. And start to run again to keep up the disguise.

I catch up to two guys sitting on the bank, one of them rubbing his foot. I better look out or I won't be last. I slow down.

> Hi.
>
> Hi. Anything to get out of the house eh? says a guy my age, but he's wasted half his life exercising.
>
> Nice clouds, I say.
>
> Yeah, they got the life. Just sit up there and get blown along. (I don't think he said that. He didn't strike me as smart enough, but he should have.) The other guy was taping his heel.
>
> You gonna keep going?
>
> Yep.
>
> Well, I'll see ya.

We'll catch up in a bit.

I amble off thinking, good, I can still be last. Actually what this race is for me is Norwegian whist when nobody bids and the winner is the one who takes the fewest tricks. That's my game.

I make my turn down the road allowance. Even the dust has settled now. It's like the old prairie here, and I think gravel, broken windshields, road graders. Gosh I remember...and then somebody's getting out of the ditch in front of me and back onto the track. A woman. What do I do? Better talk to her and not go too fast. She'll get bored with me and start running.

Hi, run outa gas?

Just picking some prairie lilies. Aren't they beautiful?

Yeah. Orange. I, uh, thought you weren't supposed to pick prairie lilies.

Well...we don't want them just to waste.

Early thirties and not beautiful but beautiful enough, slim as a boy, freckles from here to there, and red hair cut short. That's a shame. Flying a tattered flag. You could see why she picked the tiger lilies, they matched.

Your flowers'll die before we get to the finish line.

Oh I think they'll have water at the next pit stop.

Right. How soon is that?

One more bend.

You've done this before, I say, and I have to run now to keep up.

It's my fifth year.

Her marriage is that bad I think.

How come? I mean you're almost last.

I do it to raise money for the Crippled Marriages Association.

Right. That's what the race is for. CMA.

You reckon they need the money?

Well I crippled three marriages already so it's only fair.

I've never been in a conversation like this before.

Were they all yours?

Mostly.

After the last one you cut your hair.

How did you know?

Just an old dream.

I'm doing okay at this. But it doesn't help my running. Puff, puff, puff.

Are you tired? Do you want to sit down a moment?

Yes, I say, yes. I'm not a runner. I'm more of a sitter actually. If they want to make real money they should have a sit down marathon.

Or a lie-down race, she says.

Right. And I mumble to myself singles or doubles.

What?

Singles or doubles. For a lie-down race.

We're doubles.

My court. So what I do is look right at her. That doesn't sound like much but it's a real step for me. She smiles. I mean, she smiles.

Why are you running?

Trying to win an argument.

Who with?

My wife. It's uh, that she thinks that I only think of myself so I decided to run, which I hate, to make money for a good cause and that'll prove that I'm really nice and that I'm selfless. And win an argument.

But, she says, her small mouth opening and closing, your marriage must be crippled if you're going to all this trouble to win an argument, so you're probably just collecting money for yourself. So you're selfish anyway.

I had to break the story off because I didn't know what to say. Or do. If I'm not doing something perfect for a change what's the point? I thought that to be perfect you should do what you loathe, hate and detest the most, like running. For a good cause. But if the good cause is me then, well, how can it be good, like she says, like, if...so now my mind's gone like I'm arguing with my wife and I feel like a boilermaker inside or like I'm trying to sort out the Thirty Years War. That's what I get for talking with a woman. She's looking at me.

You okay? I was just joking.

How can you joke about it?

Marriage?

Yeah.

I've had a lot of practice. Would you like to run some more?

Might as well.

I don't even care if I don't lose now.

Can I run just a little behind you? I ask her.

How come?

Keep my eye on you. See how it works.

What the hell.

See how it works? Is that supposed to be humour?

I thought it might be.

And I thought you couldn't joke about things like that.

I can joke about sex. It's marriage that's serious.

Maybe we can have a laugh or two later.

So I start to think of the different kinds of laughs and which ones I like best when I hear footsteps and the two guys have caught up.

Told you we'd make it.

Don't let us hold you up, I say, there's more runners around the bend.

He's a walker, lady. Want to run with us?

Would you like a tiger lily? she says.

Huh.

Awkward pause.

Bye, she says and they run off like a well-oiled machine. People trying to be as efficient as machines. Assembly line of human beings on the run. Call on General Ludd to stop

General Motors.

What are you thinking of, she says, so I tell her and she laughs and says let's go to the finish line so we can start something, and I follow her like I said I would.

It's like being on the riverbank was. New worlds. Crickets for instance, I can hear crickets. And the faint hum of traffic. There's a small plane to the north like a dragonfly buzzing. Purple flowers in the ditch, that's the clover we were lying in. Puff, puff, puff. Nature tired in leg and side. She's forgotten me and is slowly gaining. Nothing I can do. Round the corner comes the lemon stand. I gotta stop and walk. I don't even think I can make it walking. Napoleon going to Moscow. I'm light-headed and it isn't love. She has a drink for me. I smile, I think. I wonder how far she can see inside me. The dead muscles, the never-used and now screaming muscles. I might die at the finish line. Wife, take that. Or lust, can she see...yeah, probably.

She has a fistful of tiger lilies in wet paper.

Are you tired?

No, I'm dead. I got jogger's cramp. You go ahead.

You still want to finish last?

I ain't got no choice no more.

Even my words are tired. She doesn't run and we both walk and the sun comes back. Or I can see it again as the pain goes down.

What do you do? I ask her.

Pardon me?

I mean for a living.

Oh, that. I'm a suburban counsellor.

You mean you go and talk to suburbs that have traffic problems or low density or things like that?

Well, I do talk to people

Yeah. What about?

Well, if you want to...here goes. Many contemporary problems are a result of our built configurations and in particular urban sprawl which has resulted in an immense amount of isolation, especially for women locked for a great part of their lives inside their own houses.

Was this the woman I'd just fallen in love with?

We call it the lawn chair syndrome – since their pleasure comes so often from inanimate objects and since the pursuit of beauty, in this case a tan, is a central preoccupation, though it is a rather sterile beauty since it is so little used.

So you got married three times.

Well, yes.

Are you getting closer to city centre?

All the time. Well, counselling a return to life for the suburbs is my main line of work. I'm a kind of human city planner. The men suffer most often from a disease of the automobile. They're very nervous of sidewalks and it can take a major act of will for them to mow their own lawn. Many buy tractor mowers they can climb onto from their deck. So I teach them to be spontaneous, to relax, to touch the earth.

Run in marathons.

If you were one of my clients I should be very impressed with you. You even lie down on the earth.

That's the easy part of the marathon.

I work for the provincial government. It's a new outreach program entitled the Suburban Living Renewal Program. SLRP.

You're putting me on. The suburbs get enough done for them. There's no program....

You have to keep up....

Sandy.

Pardon?

Sandy. That's my name, I tell her.

Sandy. That's nice. Sandy. You've got to keep up. The world is changing. Today's needs demand today's solutions.

She's starting to sound like a teachers' seminar.

Look....

Red.

Red?

Red. It's my name.

Red, okay Red. And suddenly I get all excited again. I mean, Red, now that's a word, not like Suburban Rehabilitation or what bloody ever.

Red. Jesus what a name. It gets me all excited.

What the hell, I don't care if I'm first or last anymore or if there's even a race.

What about my professional identity? Miss Brewster.

Can't I have one with the other?

Life just doesn't work like that.

She's getting scary. Even the wife wouldn't pull that one.

Can't you laugh about your work? It sounds funny enough.

I take my work very seriously.

Her words sound like they're dressed in tweed.

If I took history seriously – I'm a history teacher in a high school – I mean it's so serious already you'd go crazy, so you, I mean I see you're trying to make the suburbs live, but your own job, you make your own job sound as dead as a crescent. I mean a mowed lawn's got nothing on your mind when you get that glow of professional belief. I mean look at this place.

And by now we were on the last leg of the run, right through Lakeview Heights or Lakeside View or Lakeshore Vista and all the houses were colour-coded a kind of tasty off-brown with an anarchic yellow door here and there. They've even developed a new grass turf that comes in green/brown or green/yellow, and green/gray, called chocolate, lemon and cedar grass and they've begun to spray paint the most obnoxious trees.

City planner heaven, I say, and a woman with a run like yours, I mean I've been watching from back here, and a name like Red, shouldn't talk like this place. Um, I'm sorry but....

She stopped running and sat down, bit her thumbnail absently, her eyes staring through the giant tasty houses. She didn't look at me, got up and started to run. Me too. There were other tired bodies like mine settled at the side of the road now so I might not be last but what the hell. There's more than one finish line.

Hey Red, wait up, Red, I'm sorry.

It's all right.

Hey, say Sandy again the way you did.

Don't be silly.

Anyway we're doing the right thing.

What's that?

She's interested.

Running to get the hell out of the suburbs.

Sandy.

Yes?

Um, uh....

Then there's a lot of ums and uhs and we sort of finish a sentence or two in three or four hundred yards and I can hardly keep up but the upshot is I think she wants us to become, well, uh, um, lovers, and I do my ums and say I've a wife and try and close my mind from the immediate or short-term future and she says well, I've got to run now, and does.

And I slow to a walk and try emptying my mind since closing it didn't work. Nice sun, eh. Count houses to go to sleep. Monday's class and Tuesday's dinner and Wednesday's gardening and Thursday's followed by Friday and God almighty the wife has nice breasts but there's been seven days to the week for years and I'm no bargain either. Am I, I think, am I running away from it all? Or walking as the case may be. I start to sing to myself "It's only a paper moon." Singing. Next I'll go to a weiner roast or a waterslide. Next I'll get a jersey with numbers and start exercising and cut down on my drinking. So love or whatever is going to be a real pain. Clump, clump, puff, puff. Stitch in my side again. Bloody women useless as.... Mind's running down again. Terrible thing to be stuck in your own mind for your whole life. Puff, puff, puff. And I'm only walking. On my way to....

To make a long story short, or less long, I get to the finish, and I'm 479th and they think I might be the last one to finish so I win sort of and my mind is as empty as all outdoors and there she is cool clean small neat, tiger lily, sweater tied round her waist like she was still a teenager, bandana on her red hair like a bit of gypsy and she looks like a football game in October with rye and ginger in cut glass after in the last slant of summer and I say hello but I don't want to talk or move, let the whole thing petrify right now it'll never be better oh no she's going to talk and it'll start up like a marathon run you can't get out of.

Well?

Pretty well.

Do you want to go home with me?

I don't know.

Do you want to change the way you live?

Yeah.

I saw a movie where a cop in a big American city said he kept alive in tough situations by pretending to be as small and invisible as possible.

On the other hand, I decide to think, I am going to get laid by at least one of them tonight. With an athletic record like mine it should be easy.

Round the Corner

So today I think, right now, right out of the blue, it's time to turn a corner, yknow, take a chance. Who knows what's there. Maybe nothin. Like around this corner. Nothin. A nice old Caddy but that don't count. Find a girl, now that would be neat. I knew I'd go round this corner. The Royal Crest, the local where I kill afternoons. Still, if you start drinking early enough you got a better chance to go farther. Everytime you take another drink somethin might appear. Sitting still and turning corners. Drink by drink, with friends or on your own, just thinking. About Doris, about Doris, about Doris, fucking up my mind.

A good corner is not like where you come from. Not at all like a hometown. In your town you turn a corner and it's the same place, yknow same thing. Turn another corner, same thing. I swear they got a manufacturing plant somewhere turns out towns in cans and they ship them out and people get a can opener and open them up and presto there's your town. Machine made. You turn one corner you've turned them all. But not in a city, man. You gotta live in a city.

Hey Jerry, Jerry.

Yeah, what, oh hi. Bonnie, hi. Didn't see you.

Where you going? You look like there's nobody home.

Yeah, well, how are ya?

Easy to look at, hard to get.

Yeah, right, uh, nice day, like....

Last of the great conversationalists.

Not bad. 6 outa 10.

Nicer than that. It's really nice....

Sun's too hard on my complexion.

Looks okay.

Thanks a lot.

What you doing?

Well, mostly I'm standing here talking to you.

Yeah, me too. I mean to you, talking to you.

I figured it out speedy.

I'm a useless mind out loud. A real woman and I'm tongue-tied. Bonnie's too big sorta but she's as much of a corner as I'm likely to see up close these days.

Uh...

Uh yourself.

Wantogoforadrink?

What kinda drink you got in mind?

Well, uh, coffee?

Nah, you shouldn't drink coffee in this weather.

Sun's too hot.

Yeah? I didn't know that.

You get sunburn of the stomach.

I didn't know that.

Beer is a coolant, eh.

Heavy beer.

Why heavy beer?

Well you said a coolant and heavy water is a coolant for a nuclear reactor so I said heavy beer. God am I boring.

Oh, I never knew that.

There's the Royal Crest.

That's where I'm pointed.

How do you keep from lookin real eager. I guess if you're tongue-tied it's easy. Suddenly I can't think of anythin but Bonnie. Just like that. I know in my bones I got to keep cool though.

No swinging doors, just one big heavy brown one I open and she says Thanks Sir. The bar is dark wood with tables at one end and booths at the other end. We take a table. The place is mostly empty. The waitress comes round with a change purse ridin her hip and asks what we folks want and I say how bout a pitcher of beer.

I'll lose my lovely figure.

No you won't. You'll just add to it.

I talk better in beer parlors. That warm beer smell is my home and I can relax. We get the beer and I pour glass one.

Why aren't you working? she asks.

Day off, I say. How bout you?

Night shift last night. I got off at noon.

Back at work tonight?

Night off, she answers, night off.

So. She's a nurse's aide. We talk about the hospital. I pour glass two. Great thirst from all that heat.

So where's Doris?

Who?

Who my eye, she says. I thought you two were thick as thieves.

Yeah, well, we broke up.

How come?

I look in my beer like it's a lake and I can see a long way down. I do that to prove I'm a deep guy who is so sensitive he can't put into words what he really feels.

How come?

She wanted me to marry her. And I liked her but when I thought of living with her for the rest of my life I got cold feet.

She's so scrawny she couldn't even have warmed them.

I let that pass. I thought of her as slender, like all the ads for women for whatever or magazine covers.

She wanted to marry you, eh?

I didn't like the way she emphasized you but I let it pass.

What did she do, propose?

Pause.

And you said no?

Well, she had another guy too.

I pour pitcher one, glass three and swivel round looking

for the waitress with the change purse and the tray floating out in front of her and signal another pitcher. I didn't much like that last corner but at least it was new. After four now and some of the office crowd coming in and some old pensioners from downtown apartments – rat warrens really but better a rat warren downtown than a house in the suburbs. That's my feeling. All those suburbs are like hometowns anyway. Just a different manufacturing plant and they don't come in cans. They come in boxes. Here comes that Len creep, who the hell....

> Hey Bonnie, where you been? You're looking great.
>
> Len. Long time. Hey, you never phoned me.
>
> I know. Apologies most deep and heartfelt. I got posted to Toronto for a short course.
>
> 40 cents? Or wasn't it first class?
>
> Oh Jerry are you here, didn't see you. You still working?
>
> As little as possible.
>
> Sounds like you. Hey Bonnie, you're looking great.
>
> I practice every day in front of my mirror.

And I'll swear she begins to look even better at this very moment.

> Listen hon, I'd like to stay but I gotta join my table. Doing a bit of business and a bit of pleasure at the same time. You come over for a drink when I give you the high sign. Got the client in the bag.
>
> Still in advertising, Leonard?
>
> Sure am. You still the best educated caretaker

on the west side?

I'm still a caretaker.

Bonnie, I'll see you. You're looking great.

She smiles at him like she's trying to be in one of his travel-off-to-the-sunny-southland ads or buy pussy stoppers and fly around the blue heavens like a seagull. I watch him settle in his alpaca jacket or what bloody ever and what he does not do is order a pitcher of beer. His drink, after smiling the brassiere off the waitress, comes with celery sticking out the top of it. Or a zucchini. Or a carrot. Or a turnip. I hate them fuckin vegetarian drinkers. Bonnie pours. Pitcher two, beer one.

Whataya see in that jerk?

Think he looks real nice. Don't you like his suit?

Where's his briefcase and his laptop. He oughta do the whole cheese. Where'd you meet the jerk? I thought you had taste.

None of your business, Jerry. Drink your beer and cool down or I'll walk out. And hey hey hey, who's that now? Isn't that your anorexic girlfriend?

She ain't an anorexic, she's Canadian.

I've never seen anyone that thin. You could spit through her anywhere.

She's okay.

Come on. I wanta know. Scientific curiosity. Whatya see in somebody that thin?

Drink your beer and fat up.

Yeah, I know, I'm a bit lavish. I admit that. But you might as well get your money's worth.

More room in the bed.

Huh?

Skinny woman. Leaves you more room in the bed.

So sleep alone.

Yeah, I guess, yeah. I been doin it.

You ever take her out in a windstorm?

And there's Doris with her A1 smile giving us the greeting. She's slender but her lips aren't. They're like old-fashioned sofas, a place to sit on and a place to lean on. I give my best rueful grin, the one that may or may not convey everything. And I pour, pitcher two, beer two.

Hey, I'm talking to you. She ever blow away? You ever lose her down a crack?

I held on.

I'll bet you did.

Hey, hey, hey, just drink your beer and mind your own business. And drink up, you're falling behind.

And she does and we round the next corner as equals. Now who the hell is Doris sitting with? Some guy with a beard like he's read the Old Testament, twice. We sip awhile, steady as she goes, the wheels rumbling beneath us, Antigonish, Antigonish, Antigonish, emphasis on syllable one, Antigonish. That's the sound Canadian trains make. Antigonish, woo woo.

Hey, you like this train? I ask her.

Huh?

It's the super continental roaring through town.

You crazy?

Good thing we got a seat in the bar car.

You got something in your beer I don't have?

See that town? Gone. Get ready for another one. Going, going, gone.

Jerry, you out of practice drinking?

Just getting into it eh?

If you can't beat em join em.

And she takes a major swig and I pour pitcher two, beer three and signal the waitress with the change purse and the magic tray for another jug and we travel on.

We travelling day coach? she asks.

People's day coach all the way.

Len would have bought a compartment.

Leonard would have taken you on a boring aeroplane.

Doris is daycoach?

In that dress. Are you kidding? She wouldn't be caught dead in daycoach.

Hi honey. Just put it right there.

It's the red-breasted waitress with a pitcher of gold and before I get my money out Bonnie pays the lady and tops them up.

So you like em thin?

Well, sure, but other ways too.

You like em fat?

I don't know what to say. I mean it's tough sometimes, know what I mean?

You look really good, I say. Uh, do you like being a nurses' aid?

Do not change the subject. Do you like em fat?

It's a trick question. I know it is. Like I mean she ain't

skinny but she ain't entirely fat. But if I say I like fat she'll be mad, right? And if I say I don't she'll be mad, right?

Jerry!

Yeah.

Beer loosens my tongue so I can talk to people but like sometimes it clogs up my mind too and there's nothin but buzzin inside.

Do you like fat women?

I like em best when they're in between, like you.

She grins, gets up, comes round to my side and kisses me. Geez. It's like kissin a brewery but it's a nice soft brewery. I kiss back and just as we're going round the corner together I see Doris out the top of my eye.

Hi. Am I interrupting something?

Nothing much, says Bonnie, straightening up. She still has to look uphill at Doris. I haven't had the pleasure, she says.

Uh, Bonnie I'd like you to meet Doris. Doris, Bonnie.

It's a real pleasure, Bonnie.

Yeah.

You're in red again, Doris, I say.

Yes, do you like it? And she does a turn around.

Well, says Bonnie, you won't get run over in traffic.

Oh you're very funny. Isn't she Jerry?

Very funny.

Jerry, you're not drinking beer again are you?

You'll put on weight. Won't he, Bonnie?

Bonnie has her glass in her hand and drinks it down.

Yeah. You want a glass of beer, Doris?

Oh no, I don't....

She only drinks low calorie Scotch, I add

Bonnie puts her arm on my shoulder. Proprietor.

Where'd you get the lovely pedal-pushers, Bonnie? I didn't think you could buy them anymore.

Yeah, they're back in style.

Oh isn't that interesting. How do you know?

Read it.

Oh, where?

Farmers' Almanac.

Oh I don't read that.

You buy a pair of slacks and cut them off at the knees.

What do you do with leftovers?

Make brassieres for girls with small breasts.

I'm enjoying this. This is great stuff. Come on Doris, your turn. You can turn an insult with the best.

Well, Jerry, it was nice to bump into you again but I have to go back to my table now. Come and join us if you get bored.

Will do, Doris. You're sure lookin good.

And she gave me the fat lip smile I used to follow anywhere, everywhere, anytime. A grade A smile.

No wonder she's anorexic. Everything runs out her mouth.

You say something Bonnie?

She looks like a long red worm. Or a slug. Great slug-a-bed.

Jerry!

Okay, okay. Take it easy. Listen I got an idea.

What?

Have another beer.

What's the idea?

That was it.

What?

Have another beer.

Ahh.

And I pour pitcher three, glass one, but who's counting. A long pause. Feels kinda free. Gives the tongue a rest.

I got an idea too. I got an idea of what I'd like, she says. Do you know what I'd like?

What?

I'd like...us to be having our first beer right now. Start all over. Whatya say?

That makes me sad.

Me too.

And there's another pause while we examine closely what's in our beer.

What would you like? she asks.

You shouldn't ask.

Why not?

I'd like you.

There, it's said. I examine the table now, the collection of round wet stains. Looks like one of those atom models in chemistry. I look up. She's looking dead at me. With her serious eyes on. I should have stayed cool. Say nothing and you can still keep hoping.

Me too.

O my, O my. Did she really say it?

You want yourself?

Me and my mirror. No. You.

You like your mirror?

Go round all the corners you can. Be careful. It's right there.

Not first thing in the morning. Right now I feel okay. Probably because I've got a skinful of beer.

Oh oh, skinful of beer reminds me....

How do I look to you?

Great. Listen, don't go away. I'm full of piss. Hold tight, I'll be right back.

There's a corner for you. Love talk to beat anything. Doesn't matter. First things first. Couldn't hold on, love or no love. Get to the good part and your bladder betrays you. Men have smaller bladders. Weave through the tables with care. Don't upset the water table. Walk with care. If you drink don't walk fast. Setting my legs a little further apart to keep track of myself. Balance is all. And expectation. Hi Doris. Charlie. Scot. Oh this is gonna feel good. Lo Leonard. Sarah. Love to chat but I'm on an errand of mercy. Behind these swinging doors. Sssssssss. Ss. S. Ooooooooo. I am a happy man. So little does it take. What if I never go back? Right now just walk out the back door. Travel all over the country for years. New towns new people. Walk into the very mind itself. On the mental side of the street. God. We said the four letter word. Love. No we didn't, we didn't. Escape is possible. Will I have to talk to her for weeks? Listen to her for weeks?

Body talk all over the place. Hi Leonard. I am nonetheless walking light and nimble. Lo Doris. Ain't he sweet, dressed so neat. Hey wait a minute. Wait just a doggone minute. I got an idea. Must be the beer.

Doris, I got somebody you just gotta meet.

Jerry, I'm busy talking to my friends. This is....

Pleased to meet you. Cmon cmon cmon. This is really important.

And I take her by the arm. My hand goes all the way round.

She'll be right back folks. Good to meet you all.

Jerry, you are just awful.

Smile that smile babe, he's a beauty. Leonard, I'd like to introduce you to Doris.

And he sees her and gets up, not even drunk the sonuvabitch.

Leonard, this is an old acquaintance of mine, Doris. Doris, Leonard, who's just back from Toronto and deals in advertising. Leonard is a vegetarian who puts celery in his liquor. So you'll be safe.

Jerry, you always were a dope. Doris, I'm delighted to meet you.

I'm pleased to meet you, Leonard.

First name basis already.

Would you care to join us for a moment?

Well, I am with people but I will for a moment.

La de da. And I'm on my way. The great matchmaker. In piss-good health. And got rid of that Leonard. Grin grin grin on my way back through the jungle of tables. Trying to find the anchor and there she is with her big grin and she gets up and holds my chair for me.

You're a real gentleman, Bonnie.

You're wonderful.

Yeah, you're right.

Look, they're into it.

You're not jealous my old flame is going after your dream man?

I've never been out with Leonard and I'm glad you've ditched your old flame.

Never gone out with Leonard?

Well, I feel stupid.

No. It was Marty, you know that, and other guys.

And she pours on that note. Marty, our second baseman. Cup of gall. Pitcher three, glass three. End of me. I feel like I been run over. She purses her lips.

You okay?

Don't talk for awhile okay.

Hey, Jerry. She puts her hand on my arm.

I'm okay. Just like some breathing room. You know. Just....

Okay. That's okay. I'll go to the ladies.

Hand on the chill glass. Cool on the forehead. Bonnie Bonnie Bonnie. Watch her weave the tables. Walk walk. God can she walk. Her ass looks like her cheeks are holding a conversation with each other. Or chewing gum. She kissed me. Been kissed before. She's talkin to people. Who's she talkin to? Who is that guy? Dark corners to this bar. So dark they could go forever. Drive out of here and hit the highway west. Right into sundown and right out again the other side. Mountains and mountains and the long slide to the sea. Vancouver and all those flowers. Yeah. Big deal. Go home maybe. One elevator and eight street lights and wind all summer long and some lady complaining her cat's missing or the toilet's plugged. Lonely, I'm lonely as I've ever been. You can curl up in loneliness in your own backyard under the half-assed trees. Here comes Bonnie. Here comes her front. Pointin her way to the future. Who's she talkin to now goddam it. Smilin at me and I turn up the corners of my mouth. We've turned so many corners we're gettin all tangled up. Maybe that's what it is. The four letter word. Can't find your way out. Sippin slowly golden beer. Feel it goin down muh throat and into muh stomach like it's neon and I'm all lit up. She's back, she's back. Not sayin a word.

So, what's Bonnie short for? Bonofsky. Bonnard. Bonnert.

Just Bonnie. My mom thought it was cute.

Mom's have a lot to answer for.

Yeah, I never liked it. My second name is....

Bonnie Rabbit.

I went out with one guy who called me Bon.

Bon in the oven. She was only a baker's daughter but you oughta see her bons.

You were better when you weren't talking.

So we go back to it. Nothin. Long pause. Nothin goin on in my head. Here on the face of the earth and in the flow of time. She absently empties the pitcher.

Hey, I say quietly, I just read a book by a Polish writer, Czeslaw Milosz.

Seesaw Mellows?

Listen. Czeslaw Milosz.

Coleslaw Mildews?

Hey, be serious for a moment.

I've been serious before. It got me into a lot of trouble.

Anyway, Milosz says....

You've been reading again, Jerry.

Yeah, but I promise not to do it in front of you. Anyway, he says we're living right now at different times in history.

Huh?

Like I mean different people are at different times in history.

Yeah. So what does that mean on Tuesday?

Well, I think what I want to think is you and me're alive a long time ago, like when love was....

You said the word, Jerry.

See, there you go. You're being right now and what I want is for us to be alive long ago. Like in the nineteenth century.

So?

So we could say...love. And...uh....

Like before I went out with Marty.

Uh. Yeah.

She's looking me in the eye.

You wanta kiss my hand like in the movies?

And I do. In the Royal Crest. I feel stupid. I hope nobody's lookin. Then I think maybe it'll all be the same. Just another girl. Corner I been before. More cans.

Hey, I just thought. Do girls come in cans?

No, guys do.

Huh?

Like basketball players and hockey players.

Oh. Yeah.

You haven't said anything to me that's nineteenth century yet.

Well, I don't know how to say it. I think that, uh, you could be on a pedestal.

Dressed or undressed?

Uh.

I know what you're thinking, Jerry.

Yeah.

Let's go.

There's still beer....

Fuck the beer.

God I'm happy to be me, turning this corner man, with Bonnie, great hours coming, maybe more.

Dead Soldier

Some days are so hot you think they'll never end. There's so much life, so much growing. You can imagine sidewalks sprouting more sidewalks or the bricks on the old hotels taking three weeks off at the lake to cool down. You're so aware of yourself, of everything you do, like taking a step or turning your head, the kinds of things you ordinarily never notice. But in hot weather every move counts. You can taste your own sweat, feel how dry your mouth is. You seek out every bit of shade and every bit of breeze. And you get so thirsty, thirsty as hell.

Too damn hot to work, Bernard, too damn hot.

Cannot mark essays in this weather. Unfair to our students.

Right, you're right. Good thinking.

Like the rest of the university the cafeteria wasn't air-conditioned. It smelt of noodle soup and french fries.

What're we gonna do?

Go swimming at the river? Not bloody likely. We were intellectuals.

> The poor *Bridge at San Luis Rey* almost collapsed under the heat this morning, said Bernard. Poor thing.
>
> I was okay. I was in Egypt with Cleopatra. I said the weatherman and the university were recreating conditions in Alexandria.
>
> My students kept falling off to sleep, poor things.
>
> This coffee's only making me hotter. If that's possible.
>
> Too early for the beer parlour, Robert?

Of course it was but the heat was an argument we couldn't resist.

> It's so hot there's just no choice.
>
> Certainly there's a choice. Man has always a choice. Free will.
>
> Preforordestination. Predestined to drink.
>
> Free to choose in which licensed premises to do so.
>
> Toss you to see who buys the first round.

We left word with friends and took a bus downtown. And entered a beer parlour, the only oasis in town, by two. Where did we drink that July day in 1960? The King George, plain tables and chairs in a huge room with a high ceiling that was the only remnant of the grandeur of what was once the premiere drinking room in the premiere hotel in town, built like almost everything else in Saskatoon in the great prairie boom year of 1912. Four years before prohibition. Saskatoon voted dry by ten to one in July

1916, a temperance city at last. They probably hadn't redecorated the place since.

Or did we go to the Queens? With animal heads on the wall, moose and deer, to break the heroic space, and a fireplace in a corner under a low roof with cedar shingles on it and there was a rumour they'd even lit it once. We thought of it as an English pub. Or the Empire, low-roofed so it was an old space redone and wicker chairs and some nights we knew half the people there. When the bartender came round I held up four fingers and we were served two draft each, 10 cents a glass. The only other choice was bottled beer. We always ordered draft because it was cheapest and two because the law allowed two. It didn't allow much else. It was one of our favorite topics.

You can't drink in your front yard you know.

In your own house you can.

Nope. Well, in your own house, yeah, but not in your yard. Because other people might see you and then it's a fifty dollar fine. For drinkin in public.

I cannot believe it, said James, an import from England. It's like the middle ages here. Barbaric.

If you can be seen drinking you can be fined. So in your own house okay, and a hotel room, but not even in your backyard.

What if it had trees and you could not be seen?

Shit, I don't know. I guess you could get away with it.

Liquor is held in low esteem, said Bernard, that's why we drink in such holes. It's a very puritan country. Pleasure is suspect so it lives in dark places.

Like women.

They live in dark places?

No, they have em.

So you know that from observation?

I read about it.

Yeah but what about that. No women allowed in beer parlors.

Good lord, said James, that's absolutely Victorian.

The bartender came round and told James to take off his hat.

Pardon.

Take it off or out you go.

What a preposterous place.

Another fifty for that one.

What.

Wearing your hat in a pub.

You can't sing either, James. Another fifty.

You can't sing?

Against the law.

It would be a form of pleasure and you can't be too careful. You never can tell where pleasure might lead.

Sex.

See, he said it.

Can't stand up with a beer either.

Will it lead to sex too? I mean I don't for the life of me....

Revolution. Standing and drinking.

You can't carry your beer to another table either. Fifty bucks.

So we're to stay in our separate little cells and not get together because the kind of people who would drink in holes like these must be the worst kind of people and you would never want them to get together. Right?

Whenever, said Bernard, seven or eight of you are gathered together in my name, be it Red Ribbon or Boh or Pils, society must act.

I mean, said James, I have never heard of anything so ludicrous, so Victorian, so fucking stupid, plain fucking stupid.

Another fifty, Jamie.

What for now?

Swearing in a licensed premises.

Well of all the fucking....

Uh uh.

When you don't have many customs, you're proud of the ones you do have. We were proud of Saskatchewan's drinking laws. Which were wonderful in their way. They were a perfect enemy and a great stimulant to conversation. They proved that we were more intelligent than the men who ran the province. They drove us towards the excesses they were so against. James passed with flying colours. His indignation was our pleasure. Maybe he'd been to Oxford but we were a good deal more sophisticated and cool about the ways of the drinking world than he.

Why did we drink so much? Society was against it and we wanted to be outsiders. And we liked each other's company. There was so much to say and beer kept the words going. We talked of everything. Of life and death. We were all on the road to death, we said, whatever we do on the way, however fast we write or well we write, however hard we work, or drink, it doesn't matter, shoring beer and words against our ruin. And who is better anyhow, Eliot or Yeats?

I don't care if Eliot doesn't mean anything....

Doesn't mean? What about *Murder in the Cathedral* or *Ash Wednesday?* Meaning sticks out everywhere.

No but in *Prufrock* or *The Wasteland* I just don't care. I know they're supposed to mean things but for me it's art for art's sake. There's nice big holes in the poems, between the words and stanzas and you can walk through them.

But he's so pallid and bloodless. His attitudes, royalist, etc., etc., and the verse is so, what? Flaccid, weak, pale.

So he's like a city to me. Each block of poetry is like the block in a city. Then you walk around in the streets.

Despair, bad sex, a preposterous condescension to ordinary people. "I had not thought death had undone so many." Christ, what junk. It's terribly insulting. And so insulated. Away from life. So when he gains a faith it's more of the same, a way to stay away from life permanently.

I feel free in Eliot. I can just walk around on my own. Not like Tennyson you know where you have to accompany him wherever he goes until you could scream, he's always talking to you. Alfred

Lord Tennis Anyone.

We figured we were pretty damn smart. Smarter we knew than all our relatives we'd left and our high school friends, and our students, except one or two who were clearly going to become us, and weren't they lucky.

I prefer *The Apple Tree* to *Heart of Darkness*. Much better story.

That's one of our new colleagues speaking.

Good lord how could you? How on earth could you? They're not in the same league. Conrad's great.

His sentences are so ponderous and he's got no humour. I feel I'm being clubbed to death by him.

But it's got so many meanings, and ones that contradict each other, I said.

That's a good thing? Name one.

Like you want to tell people the truth and then you don't dare.

Okay, I'll grant you that but....

And that's after he's hated all those stupid people in society back home who stand between the butcher and the policeman ignorant of truth, fast asleep, half dead.

Like all your students.

Well, uh....

The Apple Tree is so bloody wet, said Bernard, buttercup glory and pagan emotion and her soft little body. Dreadful.

You just can't stand romance.

It's like falling into a perfume bath.

The point about literature is that it's written by someone who isn't you and readers can learn to see the world with new eyes and live in new worlds.

Are you going to go on like that?

Yeah, spare us your introductory lecture.

Golden mornings, apple blossom time. Michael, how could you possibly like it? You don't really, do you?

Don't be insulting. And one of the reasons you think it's overdone is the lushness of the country in rural England. Well none of you've been there and it is like that. There's nothing here like that. Flat and dull.

Do you agree? said Bernard to me.

I dunno. Maybe.

You're a city boy. A good Saskatchewan slough is full of life.

You've led an exciting life then.

I love "The apple tree, the singing, and the gold."

There is absolutely no accounting for taste.

You don't like it because it's so accessible, because everyone can understand it whether you teach it or not.

It's bad for employment.

Unlike your *Heart of Darkness*. Fecund and tenebrous. You need five books and a month to sort the bloody thing out.

Ah piss off, Michael.

When you got into it, really into it, because someone

said something really stupid so you had to fight back, sometimes all at once and yelling, then the beer went down when you weren't looking and the time passed before you knew it. Imagine preferring *The Apple Tree* to *Heart of Darkness,* which our favorite professor had said was the best short novel in the language. Is the English country landscape – is it Dorset? – really that lush? It's where we were all going, sometime. England. London. Where it all comes from.

People joined in ones and twos all afternoon. Tables were joined together and a small village was formed. In the heat, the incredible heat, 97 above said the American Jimmy, 97 a fuckin bove. Texas weather, man. I loves it, I loves it.

Yeah, and that's in the shade.

I feel so enervated.

Me too. What's it mean anyhow?

Look it up in your Oxford.

Webster.

Too big for Webster.

I almost died coming here over the river. It's a steam bath out there.

Guy hits a home run and turns into butter like Little Black Sambo before he gets around the bases.

No baseball talk, said Bernard, no hockey scores and no football lore. Please. I implore you.

This'll be the year for the Pocket Rocket.

How crueller than a viper's tongue a thankless friend.

Or a box score.

You hardly moved. That was the trick. Let your tongue do the walking. The sweat was hiding in ambush everywhere, waiting for the least movement. Beer flows down easy in the heat. Count your blessings.

> Best beer I ever had was workin in the brewery and when they kept us for overtime they brought two beer, ones from the beginning of the day they hadn't labelled. Hotter n hell in the bottling house because the bottle washing machine just added to everything else. The beer just melted down your throats. God. So cool. And you been sweating like hell so you're dehydrated. Didn't even feel the beer except maybe a little buzz. Best beer I ever drank.
>
> I am dreaming tonight of an old southern beer, best beer I ever drank.

That was Jimmy singing but we told him it was illegal so he wanted to do it again.

> Hey man, cool it.
>
> English farm labourers drank beer in the fields. That was their drink. Part of their pay.
>
> That's very interesting. Can you tell us another one?
>
> Know what today'll do to the crops?
>
> Know what bad crops'll do to our wages?
>
> Could they be lower?
>
> I never made so much money. I can buy a bottle whenever I want one.
>
> Inconspicuous consumption.

Had to go for a leak. Walked slow. Heat got me anyhow. Moving made a little breeze. Ooo Ooo Ooo. That felt better. Walkin back slow and straight. Look at them there. So animated. My feet walked me back.

Hey, you made it.

Good work.

Leave a cleaner place behind.

I'll race you to the bottom of the glass.

No matter what the weather Bernard was always neatly dressed, even in this heat. Pressed trousers, tan colour, a button-down check shirt, a very small check in colours more dark than light. Well-dressed in a very controlled way. The top button was undone, his only concession to summer. Most days he wore a jacket, brown suede, had worn it for years, his home away from home. I just wore whatever, so long as it didn't cost much, summer trousers, most often white, and short sleeve shirts I only bought when they were on sale. But clothes were a vanity, right? Like beauty and strength. What were clothes compared to poetry and philosophy?

Of course we talked of our students, the good ones and the bad ones. Bernard and I were happy enough with the classes, maybe because we were from the province and knew what to expect. The other teachers were imports.

> I do not think it possible to teach students in this country to write proper sentences, not necessarily fluent sentences but just correct ones. They have no sense of language and whatever one attempts meets with no response, absolutely no response. It's a waste of my time. Their language background must be simply atrocious.
>
> Ah fuck off Charles, said Bernard, and won the

language contest hands down.

Bernard liked his students, all of them, thought they were sweet, trying so hard, spent time with them, vague use of the pronoun this, comma splice, and here's a set of exercises. Bring them in Tuesday and we'll go over them. Awk and P and frag sp & p. The secret code of good grammar. Parse the following compound complex sentence. Bernard was not perfect. At least once a week in summer he taught with a terrible hangover, a hangover that would have killed a lesser drinker, like myself. And once or twice a year he taught while he was still drunk, on an all nighter, which was a terrible thing to do.

As the afternoon wore on slowly the drinkers came and went and by six-thirty when last round came there was Bernard, myself and one of his students, Harvey, older than us, as most of the summer school students were in those days. He was thirty-five, a teacher from Luseland or Canora or Unity. Most of our students were primary school teachers with one year of Normal School who needed a year of university to keep their teaching diplomas. Upgrading. First year English was the only mandatory class. Those of us that afternoon in the Queens or wherever were the province's educational quality control, and the barrier the students had to leap. Harvey was a bit on the short side and heavy, laughed a lot, was a bit effeminate, always agreeable, delighted to be drinking with his teachers. He bought a round. He laughed at all our jokes. We liked him at once. A good audience is hard to find. He had his own world to talk of too. He lived on his own in whatever town he taught in, Plenty or Canwood, and loved getting to the city in the summer. He regaled us with stories of interference by his principal, the school board, parents, the dilemmas of being effeminate, however cheerful you were, in a small Saskatchewan town.

> I'm like the spinster piano player. A curiosity. Once they caught me reading a book that wasn't on the course. What are you doing, Mr. Perlam?
>
> I'm reading a book, sir.
>
> Is it an assigned text?
>
> No, sir.
>
> Is it a religious tract? A temperance tract? A pamphlet on the Crows Nest Rate?
>
> No, sir.
>
> What is it, Perlam?
>
> It's a novel. Sir.
>
> A novel! And why are you reading a novel? On school property.
>
> For pleasure. And that was it, I'd mentioned the dirty word. Pleasure.
>
> You live alone, buster?
>
> Yes, sir.
>
> Pleasure eh. You've got nice looking girl students bud. Big in grade eight ent they?
>
> Uh, no, yes, I don't know, sir. But I've no interest in them. Believe me. Except their minds.
>
> Ya know, he got me cornered and the bugger took it before the school board eh, that me'n a book were having intercourse together, consenting adults.
>
> What was the book, Perlam? I asked.

I don't know. It was a Zane Grey. I adore Zane Grey.

So we liked him. He was a brand new flavour. He fit all our prejudices. And he invited us home for supper when the bar closed. It closed at 6:30, drink up time till 7, open again at 8. So all the drinkers would go home to wives and families and hot meals. Our day was arranged according to the moral sense of someone we'd never met. Or wanted to. But whose sense of propriety we attempted to offend at every turn. His Majesty's loyal opposition.

Where do you live?

I've a little house on Avenue C. I'm renting for the summer. Next to the ironworks.

Good, we can walk there.

And the liquor store has been placed on our direct route.

Act a God.

It was two blocks to the Saskatchewan Liquor Board Store, government run so no one else would be contaminated by dirty money. It was a plain rectangle with the liquor at one end and the customers at the other and a counter in between. It was painted pale government brown – all of them were exactly the same – and had a large floor fan that blew the heat around. We checked the wall list to see what we wanted, Chianti, wrote it on a slip of paper, signed it, paid the tariff, and got our wine in a brown paper bag. A low mean transaction in a low mean place, without ornament of any sort because of an early law against such matters. The architecture we called Saskatchewan neo-Puritan and delighted in the transaction the government had made as indecent as possible.

We walked to Avenue C. I was so aware of the heat I didn't even walk in the shade anymore. It didn't matter. Might as well do the day the way it is. Walk right into that sun, on those hot sidewalks, under the tracks at Twenty-Third, where there was still cobblestone on one road. And into the low-rise, tatty west side, built before the zoners made a place for everything and put everything into it. Non-conforming use, that's where we were, house and ironworks, printing shops and confectionaries, house and a garage, and so on, cheek by jowl. Not like the neighborhood I grew up in, which was houses only, or Bernard's farm or Harvey's town, though his was mixed use but without the anonymity that marked this mass-produced bungalow from the late Twenties. Living room, dining room, kitchen down one side, and bedroom, bathroom, bedroom down the other. Steps to walk up to the front door and out the back door. Furniture, early Salvation Army. Wallpaper on sale twenty years ago. Condition, rental for at least that long while the owner prayed for industrial growth and demolition.

Hey, this is great, said Bernard.

You like it?

Yes, I do. This is a comfortable house.

Well, you can't break anything, I said, but I liked it too.

I love this place.

That's really nice. I put the chicken in on low before I went to the beer parlour so it's ready in a jiff.

Have you a corkscrew? I wish to molest this bottle of wine.

Corkscrew, water glasses for wine, apologies. We sank into the sofa and an old easy chair, afraid we might never get out again.

What on earth is this? said Bernard.

It looked like an elephant with a snifter glass stuck in its back and stood on a teetering coffee table.

That's a souvenir. I bought it in Bombay. It's a bronze elephant with a shot glass. You really like it?

It's wonderful.

Bernard laughed his rapid, high laugh that always drew you into his pleasure.

I love it. And he rubbed it with his hands.

Do y'want it?

Me? Oh no. But it's...wonderful.

I'd like you to have it.

No. I couldn't. It's....

Yours. C'mon. Take it. I want you to. Please.

Well, all right. It's wonderful. Oh Robert, isn't it wonderful?

Wonderful, I said.

Think of someone doing that. Harvey, thank you.

That's okay. I'm glad you like it.

It's very generous.

Chicken ready in ten minutes. Hey and what kind of a lummox would bake a chicken on a day like today, eh?

Yeah, and use an oven instead of just sticking it on the sidewalk, I said.

It's a wonderful elephant. I just love elephants.

I hope you like chicken too.

It's wonderful, he said again, rubbing it all over.

Maybe a genie'll pop out, I said.

It's wonderful. Isn't it wonderful, Robert?

Yeah.

Chicken's ready.

And the boiled potatoes, peas, lettuce salad, at a card table in the kitchen with a linoleum floor and heat everywhere. The whole day an oven. Front and back door open and a bit of breeze coming through the screen doors.

It's a wonderful chicken, said Bernard. And it was. What spices? Marjoram?

Marjoram and sage and garlic, and I started it very high to crisp the skin and cooked it slow to keep the moisture. And I bought it from the Hutterites who were around last week so it's a real chicken. And there's an onion up its bum. Oh I forgot. You want some onion?

Bernard molested another bottle of Chianti. Over Harvey's shoulder I could see sky out the back door. First I could see a garage, and over that a two-storey brick factory building, and one elm tree on top of that and then the sky, a small square of sky, pale blue on top and pale green on bottom, the trembling blue-green of the sky. You knew it was all happening out there. Beautiful fires on the skyline warming the evening.

We finished the chicken and wine at nine, clearly another act a God because the beer parlour was open till ten. We couldn't turn it down. Wherever we walked in

Saskatoon at night, we circled the bar, the warm smell of draft beer, the warm colour of beer, our true neon. We walked to the Empire, always the Empire at night. I met a Communist there once. People said meet Mike Kalmakoff. He's a Communist. Howdy Mike, I said. Hello, he said, quietly enough. That was it. Of politics we knew only the songs, There once was a union maid, Casey Jones as a scab, Union Miner, and so on. That's one way we ended evenings, Bernard and Paul and I, singing along to *Talking Union.* Great songs and entirely unlike the way we'd been brought up, which was that politics were of no importance so you voted Liberal. But a real live communist. A true ornament to the bar. We joined a mixed table, intellectuals and les autres.

Where's the beaver tonight, Evans?

Dance at Avenue G.

Shoulda seen the fuckin broad I took home from there last Friday. Jesus.

Why? She have six eyes?

At least two twats.

You oughta be locked up, Evans.

Let's go tonight. I'm ina bad way.

Man she could make ya sit up. Know what I mean?

And your hair rise on your scalp.

And lift your spirits.

Make the dough rise.

Laugh you shits, laugh, but I get laid and you don't.

How dya know?

Evans, you lying bastard. You and I left the dance last week and went to the bootlegger's. Remember, asshole?

Yeah well I had a date with her later at the Shasta. So fuck you too.

That guy's indiscriminate.

He's a living argument for letting women into beer parlours.

Why?

He'd have to stop lying.

The shit's destroying the great tradition.

Leavis? I said.

Male-only beer parlours.

You just talk smart cause yr fuckin terrified a women.

It was worse than that because it could last so long. At some point in the evening I always escaped from the words for a while, let myself drift off. Conversation right next to you seemed far away, a kind of steady background noise that helped the reverie. You schemed an escape to all the good things, the ocean, journeys by railroad, dreams of being a hockey star, of girls and their softness. Your motor ran slower and slower.

Hey, Robert. Robert! Wake up.

Just gathering my strength. Lemme alone.

Bernard was holding forth on *Miss Lonelihearts,* which he'd just discovered and loved.

Oh those awful letters, they're wonderful. The girl born without a nose on her face. God.

Then the charming laugh and he'd clasp his hands together

as if trying to keep the happiness from getting away.

The language is delicious. The grey sky rubbed with a soiled eraser.

I find it just a chaos, a disorder.

Of course it is.

So it's really disturbing.

It's beautiful, that poor buggar, trying to love everyone and find Christ. All those awful people and all those wonderful sentences.

What happens in it? asked one of the others.

Well, Miss Lonelihearts, who writes that kind of column for the paper, tries to find Christ but ends up in bed with a fat lady instead, and then her crippled husband, whom he hopes to cure by a miracle, shoots him and he falls downstairs at the feet of the girl who had once nursed him back to health in the country. Her name is Betty. Isn't that perfect?

Sounds like the kind of book you guys would like.

Somebody's got to love it, said Bernard, poor little thing.

We argued and argued. I didn't much like *Miss Lonelihearts,* too black altogether. But we didn't argue to win, not really. We argued to argue. To make up the time as we went along. To be interesting. It wasn't whether you won or lost but that you played the game. Start another hare. We liked getting drunk, not being drunk especially, but getting there. The loosening of the mind, not the stiffening. Society was stiff enough. We were scheming our way out, one beer at a time. Stiff drunk was a hazard, but nobody said life would be easy.

At ten o'clock the process had to be changed again. Last round and everyone ordered two so the tables looked like harvest. It was one of the most beautiful sights we knew and we said so every night.

> Fuck, at's beautiful.
>
> Saskatchewan harvest.
>
> I do take it back. Not all customs hereabouts are barbaric. Let me put that another way. Some barbaric customs have their compensations.
>
> Yeah an we got half an hour to drink up an not just bloody ten minutes like in England.
>
> Yeah. N takeout.

A bunch of us chipped in and bought twenty-four at ten thirty. Harvey invited us back to his place, but we had our own drinking home in the great outdoors. Where we were driven by a guy who said he wasn't drunk. And even if he was, he said, he could drive just fine. It was only six blocks and there were no other cars so he got us there just fine. We parked at the riverbank, took a look around and scurried through a break in the caragana, through the wolf willow and down to a clear place just this side of the reeds that marked the edge of the South Saskatchewan River, rising in the Rockies and flowing via Hudson's Bay to the ocean. But first it had to get past us. We sang at it, we argued at it, sometimes we threw a bottle in but that was frowned on. We kept our beer cool in it. We talked about it.

> I saw a great river movie. Well, it wasn't all that

great but it was okay. Your driving reminded me of it.

Yeah, how's that? And be nice or you don't get a ride home.

Promise?

Get on with it.

Steamboat Round the Bend with Will Hays. You seen that? Anyway, this boat we're cheering for in a steamboat race on the Mississippi is losing but has a load of alcohol, just like you, and he throws it in the boiler and they go like hell and win.

I can drive no matter what. I can.

Saw it at the Daylight. An old black and white. I thought it was really good.

We were doing our outdoor drinking in the heart of the city, under the University Bridge, on the downtown side, far enough away from things so we wouldn't be heard, and so we could see if anyone, like the police, might come after us. We spent two summers in nature's beer parlour. Drinking in public, and standing up, and moving around, with our hats on, and singing. Nothing like confinement to inspire liberty.

Did you ever see *Mr. Roberts?* With James Cagney as the nasty ship captain? What a shore leave!

Did you hear about Tom Heggen's death? Another American tragedy.

He'd a been okay in Canada.

Yeah why?

He'd a never made it big in the first place.

The one I liked was *Pather Panchali.*

Harvey didn't know what we were talking about all the time, but he was mellow. Cool breeze off the river after a steaming day. Other people caught in houses that held the heat. Twisting and turning. Without a drink to their name. Poor things. Lords of night. That's who we were.

I said did you like *Pather Panchali?*

You ready for another?

Sure. Thanks.

Hey, don't throw empties in the river.

No, don't, said Bernard. Leave the river alone.

They're worth two cents each.

Somebody was an expert at opening one beer with another, a skill we admired but never learned. We were intellectuals, not mechanics.

I really like Antonioni. *L'Aventura.*

Too long for me.

Every slow minute was necessary to create a sense of loss in those people.

Subtitles?

Yeah.

Fuck it.

The old brown river. Black river at night, bars of light shaking on its surface from the lights on the bridge. Houses across the river, rich houses, mostly hidden in trees. Us just lying back listening to all the sounds, river the loudest, fast, turbulent, not the quiet sluggish thing we always saw from the high banks or the bridges. A beer bottle's throw away. The stars above are big and bright. The boys below are small and tight. I forget who made that one up. We thought at the time he was a genius.

Hyde, the honours philosophy student, must have been there, trying to drive us crazy with another shaggy dog story. Usually we held him off, with insults and false starts on other conversations, but if you weakened for a moment he had you. Boyfoot bear with teak of chan. That took ten minutes to set up. At least. We studiously never laughed. Yet our silence give the sonavabitch more pleasure. It's a long way to tip a Raree. They were awful. Excruciating. I even remember them. God. Maybe it was that night we got back at him, with a story that ended with a guy in a crow's nest on a ship and the ship lurched suddenly and he fell out all the way to the deck. What a terrible accident! Are you hurt? Are you hurt? Nah. I'm used to hardships. Harvey must have laughed. You can imagine how many hardships we put our hero through before that great ending. Hyde fought back. We resisted. We always knew philosophy was inferior to English anyway. Philosophy only had the general. English had the specific and the general. Life and the sorting it out. And beautiful lines like Bernard's from *Miss Lonelihearts,* about the grey sky that looked like it had been rubbed with a soiled eraser, or lines in early Eliot. Right?

A bottle of beer's a remarkable thing. Every time you get a new one you feel reborn. As you drink it, it gets warmer and has more taste, though you rarely pay attention to taste. You just drink it. At some point you look at an ounce or so left and think of the passing of time. Dead soldiers. Open another. They fit the hand so easily.

The breweries had just switched from the long-necked to the stubby bottles, to save space in the warehouse, we assumed, and to lay off guys on the line. Bugger them. So there were no more blondies or greenies. We liked teaching "Old Eben Flood" who held his bottle like a baby knowing that most things break.

And then it's the last bottle and there aren't any more. All dead soldiers. Thank God really. We'd done the day. You can't drink forever. The bottle does empty. Somebody drives us home, drunk as a skunk, him and us. To our separate cells. Without women. Only good thing about women when you're drinking – all kinds of good things when you're not – but the only good thing when you are is dancing. Dancing is great. You don't have nearly as bad a hangover when you dance.

Was that the night Bernard and I met the hearse driver from Foam Lake who drove us home at sixty miles an hour over the narrow traffic bridge and up the short hill and when the policeman pulled him over he said he was in a rush to get a body and he was let off. Or the night Bernard and Jeff saw the newspaper sign, tours anytime, and took one at two in the morning. And pulled the snow guard across Twenty-first Street and laid down for a nap. Or the night Bernard jumped up and grabbed a branch on a tree and it broke and he felt so sorry for it, because he loved all living things, that he planted it in a giant garbage can he dragged to his office, filled it with water, fell asleep under its shady boughs and was still there next sunny morning half an hour before he was supposed to go teach. And did. Teach. Or the night he met a salesman who sold from a railroad car and joined him for a late drink or two and he fell asleep and woke up next morning on a moving train. Got off at Warman, named after a Canadian poet, Cy Warman, a real estate and railroad poet from the Canadian Northern. Got off at Warman, hitched a ride back to Saskatoon and got into town at 11:01. One minute after the beer parlours opened. Act a God. Bernard just lived more stories than anyone else. Or he was plunging into a hundred stories to get out of one. That might be the case.

Later it was tough. To meet. I had so many other things in my head. We lived in different cities. I had a new agenda, and there's a deadly word that says a person is trying to go places. Living in a house on that riverbank. Where there's few stories. At our wedding dance Bernard gained a local fame by eating an entire ham and leading the drinking on into the night. Years later he drank too much and there was almost no process. The being drunk, not the getting there. All product and no process.

One thing you discover at the end of an elegiac beer is that – do not use 'is that' or 'is when'; always reconstruct a sentence they appear in – and isn't it nice to see a semi-colon again? – is that a moment is a moment, then as now, and they're all equal, except some are more alive than others. Some you make up as you go along. We were learning literature in the field. An ending was always inevitable and yet a surprise at the same time. Bernard's death.

Which I've just heard about in London itself. Our dream city. I'm writing this in the courtyard of a pub on an early Saturday afternoon. Two mums with a giant pram have parked six little girls and gone in for halves, of brown bitter and blond lager. The older girls look after the toddlers. The sun is shining mildly through the semi-opaline lustrous air of the great city. The kids are petting a large German shepherd who accepts their attention patiently. Through the door of what used to be the public bar I see a young man and woman playing cribbage. There are guys playing pool. One of the little girls climbs up beside me and smiles. I smile back, my hand on my pint that no harm may come to it.

How would Bernard have seen our long day back then? He wanted it as much as I did. But even after all those drinking bouts I've no idea of him really. I know his friends want to tell his stories over and over, stories he made without a thought of publication. Wringing the last drop from that incredibly hot day. And then the beer is all gone.

Hey Bobby, you want another?
Oh sure, Bernard, sure. Does a duck like water?
I saved a six pack in the trunk of the car.
Oh wow. Fantastic.
We'll go to my place and I'll play Mahler.
Great.

The Missing Girl

The world had gone absolutely still. He opened his eyes. In the heart of the city and not a sound. He lay there. He could hear no cars, no machines, no workmen. No birds and not the breath of a wind. It was uncanny. He couldn't sleep. It was as if he were in the country, the remote country, or as if the world had come to an end. He'd forgotten to wind the clock. Nothing marked the passage of time. No breath of wind. He had not yet moved. What if the world had come to an end in the night? The entire city frozen stiff. Everything was still there, like yesterday, only nothing moved. He looked down at his hand, directed his forefinger to move, and it did. He'd been spared.

He sat in the living room. Not a sound. He opened the drapes and the stone city stared back. It looked just like yesterday. The sky was light blue on top and pink on the bottom, just as if day were about to break. Over the chimney pots and TV antennas. All the windows in the terraced house opposite were empty and dark, like windows in a nightmare. The trees, the fat green trees, didn't move an eyelash. They were dead, like vegetables in the supermarket. The green cabbie shack was there, the zebra crossing, the parked cars. He assumed the air was there, between him and the window and the window and the trees. He could breathe. Where were the people, the traffic, the sound, in this huge and bustling and noisy metropolis? Would he have to invent everything? Every encounter, every sound, every step of the way. The refrigerator did not hum, nor the gas heater, no noise from the usually bustling alley. He rubbed his small growth of beard and heard the noise. Thank God. And waited. Slowly his ears filled with silence, which has a small motor of its own, a kind of buzz that's always underneath everything else. You must listen closely to silence, pay attention to that motor – is it in the head? – which turns on when all other sounds go dead. When the summer world is frozen stiff in a nuclear deep freeze there is still this low buzz, as if your head were a cavern and silence an ocean that washed against the walls.

He watched the trees across the road. Each had hundreds of green arms radiating out from its centre, like a petrified explosion. The petrified forest. The trees were a fountain too, a green fountain in which all the bright water was held in place forever, sweeping up and then out and then hanging in the air, waiting to fall. He could move, walk, drink, cough, and hear all those sounds. He moved his left arm and watched it fall back to his side. He swivelled his head and looked out the other window. Are the people frozen like the trees? Am I, he thought, the only person who woke up this morning? He thought of his mouth and ordered it to say hello. It did. His finger moved when he told it to. Think hard now of a bird, a bird, a bird. That didn't seem to work. He thought of a girl. That had never done any good. But perhaps now if he were the only boy in the world. But nothing seemed to come of it. Concentrate more. He thought of how they met, what she wore, how she moved. He began to invent a whole life. But nothing happened and the trees hung in the air like statues set in front of the stone buildings. Think of the refrigerator. Try something easy. He heard it. The fridge was on. He put his ear next to it. Yes, the freezer was humming its low sweet song. A local freezing to go with the general freezing. Had he started the fridge? Had he willed it to turn over? He thought again of the girl, harder than he ever had before. Let there be day, he said, and looked out the window and a sweet broth of yellow lay over the row of grey houses. Wind, he thought, and began to wave a copy of a magazine on the table. A local wind. The air can be entered and stimulated. Still, you wouldn't want to wave a magazine at every tree in town. The noise would be deafening.

Later that day he sat in the park. The world had come to life. In spite of himself he thought, for he had not willed all this. Who could possibly will all this? It was Sunday and warm and hundreds of people filled the park. There were big ones, who sat next to him on the bench, two old men speaking German. Medium-sized people walked on the wide cement path in front of him, tourists who stopped to read street guides, mothers with small children in pushchairs, young black guys going backwards on roller blades, an East Indian child with a helium balloon tied to her waist. Who could invent all that? There were small people, a long way away through the trees, playing soccer on a bright green field, or having a family picnic, or lying in the sun in bikinis, males and females. Wherever he looked movement was incessant. It could not be stopped. If you yelled Stop! no one would pay any attention to you. The trees moved all the time. The breeze was steady and the sun strong. A boy and his father bounced a soccer ball in front of him. Three Arab girls chattered like giant birds. The old men were still. Their cadence was slow and their language inexplicable. Yet in front of him the whole world moved, a thousand movements at a time. He grew tired of the incessant activity of the trees. Like maggots, like a can of worms, he thought, like a river washing over you, the park.

A van drove down the wide sidewalk and twenty policemen in white shirts and blue trousers got out and lined the walk. A German shepherd barked. People stopped to ask the police directions. A helicopter came in over the far trees with a great whirr of noise. It blanked out his mind. It landed on the embassy lawns through the trees. He wanted to shoot it down it was so loud. Shoot it down with a silencer. A policeman came to their bench and showed a photocopy of a young girl.

Have you seen her?

No.

If you do, contact us. She's been missing since Thursday.

In all of this petrified city so frantic with movement someone was missing. He shut his eyes and saw nothing but things that weren't there. He saw what he wanted. He thought of the girl. And heard the motor of the city turning over and over, constantly in motion, dizzying.

That evening the woman made him supper and wanted to talk. He thought he should talk to her. It seemed fair. If she fed him he should talk to her.

Do you love me?

This morning the world stopped.

Because of me?

I don't know why it stopped.

I think that's wonderful.

It just stopped.

That you should love me that much.

It must have been about five, very early.

Will you stay with me?

There were police at the park.

How are you?

They were looking for a girl. She was missing, a French girl. They showed us her picture, but only a photocopy.

Do you like the dolmathis?

She was very pretty.

Who?

The missing girl was very pretty.

Do you love me?

I wonder how she vanished. I wonder if something awful has happened?

He kept thinking of the girl. It was important. A missing girl. Did she fall into the silence? And never get out? Perhaps hundreds of people have gone missing today, fallen into the silence. He wanted to be in the silence again. He hated talking. He'd rather go without supper than have to talk. She'd continue for an hour. Or hours. He'd go mad. She kept asking questions he could not answer. He wanted the world to petrify again. Starting with her tongue. What a terrible thing to think. He needed the tongue, on him. But the words. Was anything worth the words? He wanted to be back in the park again, where everything was on the move all the time and you knew no one. They kept moving till your eyes and brain dizzied. But you didn't talk to them. You were not responsible for them. You said a word or two, like no to the policeman, I've never seen her. Who is she? A young French girl, last seen near Paddington, wearing jeans and a white blouse. I'll watch for her though. Thank you, sir. He liked that kind of conversation. You knew where you were. Both sides were happy. Both sides had done their duty. But this. He never knew where he was. He always felt he was about to drown. She's telling him about her day, in detail. Oh my God. But she's not telling about her day. She's sharing something, to help tie them together, to say how hard her life is now, to explain the cost of things on her one salary, to show how hard she works. Her words mean so many things you never know where you are except trapped in one room with one voice. It has to end. She goes on. He nods. Could she go on forever? He smiles at her. Perhaps she could go missing like the French girl.

Perhaps he had started the world this morning. Perhaps he could make it stop, or parts of it stop, selected portions of the world. He liked the way she looked. If she were in a picture she would be wonderful. He was thrilled to see her. But she talked. If only she were frozen stiff. Some of her stories he had heard over and over. He was going mad. Can I get you some ice for your drink? he said. He began to concentrate. Not on the girl this time. On her, the talker. The ice queen.

When he entered the store everything was for sale. They sold everything. They gave nothing away. He understood that. Were there items storekeepers loved so much they wouldn't sell them? It would be something if they gave things away. A store that was that friendly. They didn't talk except in the way of business, as a matter of necessity. Thank you, sir. What size, miss? No turmoil, no real conversation, though commotion was constant, the going and coming, the slow ascent or descent on the silver escalator. Every night the store froze. All the goods, the aisles and counters and racks of goods, froze, still as ice. The statuesque girl was here, on the second floor, in the women's section, selling things, with her smile, her easy walk, her pleated skirt. She moved slowly, gracefully. Her face was as composed in profile as a portrait. The proportions were strange, the mouth too small, each lip almost a perfect small heart, high cheekbones, the eyes placid, still, blue. He'd trailed her round the art gallery, the summer show, room after room. She was very tall, her head rather small on her body, as tall as him, and her skin an even tan colour, without blemish. She could watch a painting perfectly still, her finger touching her lips.

He decided next morning, early next morning, just after he had started the motor of the city, which sounded like the motor in his fridge, that he should spend his day looking for lost girls. He would travel down the silence. He would stand absolutely still. He sharpened his pen. He stepped into the noisy world. He slaughtered the talking woman's every word. He waited in the pitch dark, in the bright sun, pen in hand, for the statuesque girl. Let there be silence.

Get your Jive on Highway Five

Driving headfirst into summer, as fast as the law allows. Summer hot lovely and everywhere. I liked it so much I even said yes to discomforts like sticking to the seat or the wind howling in my ear.

Why don't you use the air conditioning? I'm baking.

I don't like it. Summer's summer.

What?

I said....

See, you can't even hear with the wind. It hurts my ear.

Pretend it's a waterfall.

What?

Pretend....

I heard you.

Roll up your window.

I'd die.

I ask you, how many days are we going to have over 90 in the shade? And there's hours to go yet. In the shank of the afternoon. To hell with the comforts of mild weather. I mean, this is summer.

Oh, I'm so sticky, she said and shifted her bottom.

Floor vent open?

Sure.

Pussy cool?

Yes, thanks.

I'm interested in your health.

Thanks a lot.

Radio talking to us. Summer sizzler shopping spree, Esso you make it better, somebody's giving away free hot dogs, a Bay jamboree on summer fashions, new coke and old cars, you always wanted a Cutlass, right? Saturday afternoon, 2:45, sunshine and a very warm 33.

What's that in your temperature?

What?

33, what's that?

Well, uh, 33 plus 33 is 66 plus 32 is 98, take away say 4 is 94. Hot.

Hot in my temperature too.

They hadn't taken much on the history of temperatures in her school. Radio plays Route 66, get your kicks, and this ain't Oklahoma City, Amarillo, San Bernadino, I start to sing along and she moves it to rhythm, get your kicks on route 66, get your jive on highway 5.

I got King Cole singing that.

Who?

You don't know a great deal do you?

Radio says it's love at first sight for Mr. Submarine.

You believe in love at first sight? she asks.

I believe in lust at first sight.

You're a shit.

And she's got her arm on the window, browning, absently watching the fields and trees go by. Radio talks all over the world, Ireland, South Africa, Nicaragua, Zimbabwe, Sahara, where summer is out of control. Too much of a good thing. Then you can buy 50 acres of cars and it's a good day for Kentucky Fried Chicken, brunch on the terrace, here comes Monday mania at the superstore and would you like to go to *Rambo,* Lane Brody, whoever she is, sings "He burns me up," nice title and I'm happy with a radio jingle, the Stones, furniture bonanza, it feels right to be in the middle of the buying and selling. It feels like being alive now and not some other time. For some reason, even though you know it's all crap.

Clouds coming up. Where the hell from? Are we driving out of them or into them? I hate clouds, I want to be in the eye of the sun.

Want to stop for a hamburger? I ask her.

Too hot to eat. Find a motel with a pool.

She has the various appurtenances, etc. besides youth its own self, and keeps shifting in the heat, and in my mind, whether I'm looking or not or present or not. She makes me think of all the missing people, the fires of love burning all night long, night so hot you can feel the sun from the other side of the world. Is it shining through? Like a flashlight through your fingers. That's what she's like.

She's in another room but her light's on here too.

Aren't you ever going to pass that camper? He's only doing 90.

90. What's that? 55. Okay. I was daydreaming. The passing is easy as they move over to the shoulder. Wave, wave for courtesy sake. Now there's a farmer dragging some kind of giant insect behind him.

Looks like a horror movie, she says.

Yeah and look at the bloody clouds.

Oh good, it'll cool down.

And she flaps her gypsy cotton shirt to keep cool, but the clouds have moved so fast there's not a scrap of sun left anywhere on our landscape. The clouds have obliterated focus. Of course the sun is indiscriminate and shines on everyone alike, on Dusty Bogus at home plate, on your aunt picking tomatoes, on your sister barbecuing herself evenly on both sides. But it shines on you. That's what you know. God's eye on you. A cloud can't shade on you, if you know what I mean. It's got no focus and right now we could be anywhere or anyone on any day.

Did you see *Mad Max?* she asks.

Which one?

The last one, *Beyond Thunderdome.*

Yeah.

Did you like it?

What?

I said...why don't you shut the window?

Okay, for a bit. What'd you say?

Did you like it?

I thought it was great.

Me too. I really loved it.

You like Mel Gibson?

Sure.

All he does is frown.

He's mysterious isn't he, like you don't know who he's going to be or what he'll do.

And you'd like to find out.

Yeah. Absolutely. Yeah. Who do you like, I mean among actresses?

I like that one in *Mad Max*.

Who? Tina Turner. Wow, have you got delusions of grandeur.

No, the other one, the Australian girl.

Oh yeah, well she was nice I guess. Sorta plain.

She had a great voice when she did the tell.

Yeah. Okay. Can I ask you a question? Like, why do you go to so many movies? Because, uh, there aren't usually people your age at, I mean, more my age, oh shit I just put my foot in it, didn't I?

I never get a hangover from a movie.

Hey, do you like driving?

Yeah I like driving, going, going, gone. Where the hell's the sun?

Why do you like it so much?

You ask any more questions I'm going to open the window again.

Okay, no more, just answer that one.

It's God's eye.

Yeah? I just spent three months in God's eye trying to get into the shade.

Well, you look great. Brown as a berry.

I'm gonna like showing off my tan back home.

Hey! Sunshine up ahead. Comeback of the day. Stick your arm out and get a rider's tan.

And she smiled and did. We were in a lane between cloud ranges, like in the Kootenay Valley, round a bend and into a lake of sunshine and I envied her arm getting all that experience. Here's an arm that's been places, an experienced arm to display at pit stops. Bright green light in the fields.

I'd picked her up this side of Sicamous with her thumb in the air, cotton gypsy skirt and a halter or whatever it's called and a backpack. Imagine that, a backpack. I'd never talked with a backpack girl. Later than my time. She'd been picking fruit all summer long in the Okanagan, the heart of the summer. Summerland. Going back to Hamilton she said, McMaster, sociology.

Listen, I said, you can have a ride but don't use that kind of language.

What kind?

Sociology.

I got better ones than that.

What?

Reification.

Now that's really scary.

We rose through the mountains on a hot day, lunched in a Voyageur at Golden where the trekkers had been fed I told her on long tables under the trees and thought for a moment they'd come home.

I didn't know you were old enough to know those guys.

Piss off and eat your hamburger. And hamburger. I figured you for a salad girl. Maybe yoghurt. Next you'll order liver and onions and banana cream pie.

Lay off, it's delicious.

And to prove it she took a greasy big bite and licked her lips. I shook my head and she grinned, white teeth in all that brown skin.

You could be a toothpaste ad with that set of teeth. You ever see a movie called *Smile?*

Nope.

About a beauty contest and one girl who's a veteran beauty tells a rookie to put vaseline on her lips because she'll have to smile so much her lips will chap.

Think I could win a beauty contest?

Not with that onion sticking out of your mouth.

What colour are my eyes?

I don't know.

Well, *look.*

Okay. Blue.

Yeah, see, some people never look, never even see what's right in front of them.

What colour are my eyes then?

Beady.

Thanks.

We did the Kickinghorse talking, a bit of her life, a bit of my life, sailing like a boat on the lake of summer, me driving, she water-skiing in wide bends slicing arcs of water.

Like a beer commercial. A bit of cool in the hot. Beer in Banff in some dark interior thirsty as fish and my round she said and put her hand on my wrist. Your round, my life I thought and put on my best smile and we hightailed it out of the mountains on TransCanada 1 and into Calgary.

Hey, you believe in being the centre of summer, or something like that, right?

Right.

So how come you're travelling in Canada? You gotta go south right? All those movies and....

South. You mean Mexico.

You know what I mean. The States. Like Route 66. They don't make movies in Mexico, I mean they make movies but not, you know what I mean.

What kind of marks do you get in sociology?

Watch your language.

Pouring headfirst into prairie, the summer being invented before our eyes, hers blue, mine off-brown. Sunlight on the paperback. Stones on the radio. Bare brown feet padding to the shower.

Sun climbing the mountain of the sky all day this very day which will also die but so hot the night will keep the imprint. Easing by all those cars with local Saskatchewan license plates. The local travellers on the skin of this bright green planet. Must be lots of rain this year. And we beyond the legal limit but not enough to do anyone any harm are passed in turn by a man on his way somewhere very fast. Me careful on all roadways. Anyways.

Any road. I'll be loving you always.

That motel pool at Calgary and she had a bikini in that backpack. I'm used to one-piece women. Bikini and backpack, I'm in the world again I think feeling a bit slack bellied against such competition so what could I do but dive in and let the day take over. She was happy and for my part I lifted the tequila out of my suitcase. No point being unhappy. Cheers.

Day running down and she's been asleep now for an hour. Slow down for the junction of highway 14 and she wakes up, hot and sticky.

Where are we?

Almost there. You okay?

I'm dry and sticky. I feel like I been sleeping in the dirt. You got your sun back eh?

My sun. She rubs her face. I give her one of the peaches we bought.

Imagine buying peaches. I ate enough to start an orchard inside me this summer. You gonna stop soon?

Bout half an hour.

She stretches, touches my arm.

Hey why don't we go back the other way? Huh? I mean, I'd just like to keep on going. I don't care about school. What dya say?

I had a lot of things I could say. Miles to go before I sleep, work, win, provide. Her finger on my arm.

Hey, come on, turn around. I don't care where. No wait, I'm too sticky. Find a nice motel, we'll turn around tomorrow. Okay?

She slumps down again and dozes off in the heat. Cheers.

And the Girls Came Out to Play

He shut his eyes and let the wind wash over him. It must have blown a thousand miles he figured and come from an oven. His Blue Jays cap was tipped over his eyes and he spread his legs out. Robbie Alomar's made all the difference, he thought. He could hear splashing in the pool. Olerud's on a hitting streak. Their voices were so high. Juan Guzman pitching so careful.

Hey, Ronnie.

Alomar cutting behind second base and lobbing the ball to first on the run. Beautiful.

Hey, Ronnie, come'n join us.

Yeah we need a man in the pool.

Giggles. Borders should be hitting better, but he sure can spit.

C'mon, Ronnie.

He had a bathing suit in his backpack but he didn't want

to be in the water with the three of them. They were yelling at each other again. He tilted his cap up an inch and watched them. Lynda was his girl and she looked as good as her friends. From the neck down. She was okay. She wasn't painful to look at. She didn't hurt your eyes. Okay, so she had mousy hair and her nose was too big. Her breasts were wonderful. Maybe all breasts were wonderful. He remembered the feel of them. Should he have stopped when she told him to? Lavender and Niamh were in bikinis so all he looked at was what he couldn't see. They were scary. You never knew what they'd say or what they'd do. The most beautiful girls in grade ten and they knew it. They made him nervous.

Please, Ronnie.

That was Lynda and he was leaning on the pool edge so he could see the white bulges of her breasts against her brown skin.

I don't wanta.

He's afraid of girls.

He is not.

Well you oughta know.

Shut yr mouth, Lav, or I'll shut it for you.

Yeah, you and that wimp.

Ronnie watched as Lynda dove back under water in a great white splash and grabbed Lavender's legs and dragged her down thrashing and she came up spitting water.

You cunt.

Serves her right, the stupid...Ronnie couldn't say the word and didn't want it to exist anyway. There were too many of them in front of him.

Put some music on, Ronnie. That's a good boy.

He could do that and slotted in Mack and the Mack Attack which was drums, guitar, sax and dead simple words. Even they'd be able to understand. But it was good dancing music and it drew them out of the water and Lavender grabbed his hand and yanked him up.

Hey wait, my beer.

He put it down, had his Blue Jay cap removed by Lavender and danced. He was a good dancer. Only Lav didn't want to boogie on her own, the two of them never touching or even paying attention. Lavender grabbed him round the waist only around the waist was stupid because all you could do was just jump up and down so left hand right hand and him around the waist and she on the shoulder like his mom taught him they used to and they danced fast, around and around. Her midriff where he had his hand was already warm. Her flesh gave a little. It was soft, like a pad. When he swung her away he could see the water drops running down her left thigh from the bikini. Her black hair was slick on her head from swimming and she looked almost like a boy. She kept trying to make eye contact as if there wasn't enough contact already. He wanted out of it but another slower song had started, like a blues.

C'mon, Ronnie, closen up.

He saw Lynda watching, not mad he didn't think but watching. Lav's arm went right round his neck and pulled him close so he could feel her breasts and her belly and they were both wet and he could hardly stand her on him. She opened the palm of her right hand for a shoveaway and he wanted to put the palm of his left hand on her...thing. God he wanted to. No, he didn't. He never would. Lynda was watching. He wouldn't anyway. He couldn't. He wished they'd go away and he could watch the Blue Jays game on his own. Even Lynda. He'd touched her through her panties. They'd kissed so hard last night he was afraid he'd bruise her lips and he felt her teeth. Lavender kept trying to catch his eye and breathed in his ear. Is she making fun of me? But he was a good dancer and he kept cool. He got even cooler when she leaned close as she could for the last twirl.

Lavender stood back and looked down at his crotch.

Hey, you wet yr pants.

It was wet from her bathing suit.

Musta been really excited.

He wanted to kill her, kill the stupid....

Let's get him wet all over.

That was Niamh who had towelled herself off and now charged him from the rear, yelling here I come. She gave a big push on his shoulder blades and Lav grabbed his belt but he hit her arm hard and he had his runners on so he kept his grip and he grabbed Niamh's arms and swung her into the water.

Hey.

Splash. Then he went for Lavender. Lynda was watching.

Stay away, wimp. You don't dare.

She backed onto the grass and was penned in by roses and the fence.

Lemme alone. I mean it!

Her voice was suddenly serious but Ronnie grabbed her arm hard and yanked her.

Don't hurt her.

That was Lynda, but he had started and couldn't stop. He grabbed her between the legs with his other hand so fast he didn't even think.

Don't! Please.

Threw her over his shoulder.

Put me down you fucking ape.

Carried her to the pool and threw her in as far as he could, belly flop first. Then he turned to Lynda.

I didn't do nothin. Ron. C'mon. Fair's fair.

She crossed her arms in front of her breasts as if to protect herself and he saw the full hips again, bigger than her girlfriends'. He wanted them so he grabbed her there and pulled her toward the pool. He figured it was okay to grab them in places he shouldn't because they'd started it. He could grab them where he wanted.

Ron, don't. Ronnie, please. Don't you dare.

That meant she didn't want to be left out. That pleading. That's how he figured it. He put his arms right around her waist and gave her a bear hug, hard as he could, as he walked her towards the water.

Ow. It hurts.

She was close to tears. He let her go. Lavender and Niamh had climbed out. Lynda cried. They watched. Lavender walked over to the ghetto blaster and put in Beach Bunnie. That was one of hers.

Cute music, said Ronnie, real cute.

He watched Lynda. She sat at the pool's edge sniffling. He walked over to say sorry and leaned over, only she grabbed his belt and he was off balance and she threw him in and laughed through the tears. He heard her as he went under, mickey mouse wristwatch and all, and swam like mad underwater because they'd be after him and he could hear the water explosions as they dove in, one two three, stupid tits, they should have stayed poolside if they wanted to keep him in and he swam for the diving board, grabbed it and swung himself up, one hand coming up out of the water to grab his jeans, too late. He walked off dripping down the pool edge, into Niamh's house where he found a towel in the bathroom, dried off, took off his jeans and put on his swim trunks, walked into the rec room and the big tv. Shit, it was already the last half of the fourth and the Jays were down by two runs. He watched. He tried to get rid of his mind.

Lynda came in, in her long beach shirt. He wondered if she was wearing anything under it as Sprague took a called strike three. He had his cap back on, to help the team along, looked at Lynda and put his shades on.

For heaven's sakes, Ronnie, it's indoors.

He decided she didn't exist and watched the game. She watched him and decided the game didn't exist. She scrunched up her face awful, to see if he'd take his eyes off the set, but he didn't so she did an ape imitation, got no response and walked out. He went to the bar fridge and opened another beer.

That's not yours. Lynda was still watching from the door, her head to one side, her brown legs in the sun which outlined through the shirt where her legs met. Ronnie took a swig that finished half the beer and Lynda walked out.

Hey Lav, hey Ni.

Gone. He stuck his legs out, flipped from channel to channel during the ads, found a game between San Diego and L.A., set the return button so he could flash from game to game. The girls were laughing again. He drank and settled back. Niamh came in with a towel round her shoulders.

That's my dad's beer.

Tell him thanks.

Well, we can do it too.

She opened the fridge, bent over and stuck her bum at Ronnie, took out a bottle of white wine with a screw top. Ronnie watched under the cap. She ignored him and carried it outside where the girls cheered hurrah. Good, now maybe they'll get drunk and leave me alone. He would have gone home but he was stuck. Niamh lived on an acreage and Lynda had driven them out. He could hardly stand it with them. Like how could he talk with them? They'd talk about stuff like teachers or clothes or chem lab or other guys and what they saw on tv. All that stuff. As if they didn't have that other stuff between their legs. How could you go swimming with three of those things, three pussies, three pussies and pretend there was anything else? How could you? How could you? His left hand was clenched tight.

C'mon out and have a real drink, Ronnie.

Girls' drink. He watched Carter go down swinging and went for another beer. He drank at it seriously. He was all keyed up. His heart was going to beat the band. He took another swallow. There was Lavender in the doorway in her bikini, the wine bottle in her hand. They were drinking out of the bottle. It was more than half empty. She was so beautiful, more beautiful than any girl Ronnie had been in a room with. He'd seen beautiful women, in movies, in ads, even in the mall, but never one in the same room he could talk to. He looked at her. He lifted his bottle to her. They both drank.

Lynda wants you to come out.

I'll miss the game.

You sure will.

Lavender walked toward him. He was terrified and his cock tingled. She sat beside him.

Who's ahead.

Tigers, three one.

You gonna come out.

I don't want to.

I'll tickle you.

Pick on someone your own size.

You are my own size.

He drank, looked at her. She took his shades off. Niamh yelled from outside.

Hey Lav, where's the bottle?

Hold yr horses.

Hey bottle, said Ronnie, where's the lav.

Very funny.

How many times you heard that?

About five hundred.

At least.

At least. C'mon, Ronnie. Be nice. Talk to us.

About school huh? Or Vinnie Terranova.

No. Me. Talk about me.

He flipped channels and looked at her again, her hands behind her head, her breasts stuck out. Did she do that on purpose? A tiny bit of curly black hair leaked out the left side of her bikini crotch. Her eyes were shut. So he could look.

Whatcha lookin at?

Alomar.

Huh?

Second baseman.

Yr boring. I'm going back out.

He took another swallow after she left and crossed his legs so it wouldn't show. Hard on. Boy did he have nervous energy. He was so jumpy. He couldn't pay attention to the ball game he was thinking about them so much. The girls and their stuff. Until Alomar doubled home the tying run. Yeah. Girls giggling. First place on the line. Giggles closin in my God they're comin I can't stand it. He started to get another erection. He got up quickly and crouched down behind the bar, slipping as far as he could into the large bottom shelf. And felt stupid, really stupid. It was Nih and Lynda talking.

Hey, he's gone.

Must be in the can.

Jerkin off.

That's not nice, Nih.

Yeah, it's a real waste. Right, Lynda, lover?

You shouldn't drink, you get so stupid.

And horny, boy am I horny.

Your mom and dad'll be home any minute.

Nah they'll only be on the 14th hole and they

gotta drink afterwards yknow.

In here, Lav.

All three of them, oh God, I'm stupid. Don't find me, please.

Hey, said Lav, do you exercise yr breasts? Like in the magazines.

He was growing again.

No way, said Lynda. It's stupid.

Yeah, well you don't need any help in that department.

See, the hands together like this.

Let's all do it.

I feel dumb.

You look like a retard.

Mine are biggern yours are.

Queen of the tits.

God, that was Lynda talking.

Wonder where he is?

Probly watchin us.

Ronnie wished he'd gone to the can. What if they look? What if they find me? Stupid stupid stupid. He couldn't stand himself. Stupid.

Hey Ronnie, get outa there!

Yeah, I gotta see a man about a pussy.

Niamh!

Cat, sorry.

Dog.

Oh yeah.

Where the hell is he?

Ready or not here we come.

You look outside okay?

Yeah, spread out.

Where's home free?

Right here.

Niamh!

Christ, girl, yr askin for it.

Yeah, and I'll open another wine.

I gotta drive.

More for the rest of us.

Least he ain't in the can. I gotta pee.

He heard Lav go into the can and Lynda go outside to look. That left Nih and she changed places with Lav in the can and then got another wine.

I'm takin to the woods. If I find him first I'm gonna keep him.

They're leaving. Oh God, I'm gonna be okay. Only he looked up and there were legs in front of him.

Hi Ronnie.

It was Lav looking down at him. Caught. His cock was nervous.

I knew you'd be there. Yr scared of us aren't you?

Yr so stupid.

C'mon Ronnie.

I gotta go to the john.

I'll be waitin.

He walked in there fast. Pulled down his swimsuit. He had to bend it down to aim it right. Phew. That felt good. Musta been a fifty seconder. All that yellow beer down the tube. Now what? God, she's gonna tell. I feel so stupid.

Make a fool out of me, she'll make a fool out of me. A goddam stupid fool. Stupid fool. Stupid fool. Jesus stupid fucking stupid fool. His heart was racing. He hated himself. He opened the door.

That took long enough.

Lotta beer.

Skinny water pipe.

You gonna tell?

What do I get if I don't?

Lav walked over to him, put the fingers of both hands around his neck, drew his head down, got up on tiptoes, pressed all along his body on purpose and kissed him, really kissed him and he felt his loins tingle and his cock moving again and nothing could stop him now he put his arms around her hips and grabbed her soft ass and drew her to him hard as he could his kissing having lost control it was so intense and moving all around.

She pulled back her head.

Hey, I found him!

Jesus Christ, you cunt.

They rushed in but he had already untangled himself.

Where was he?

Behind the bar.

Behind the bar?

Yeah, hiding from us. Ronnie's scared of girls.

What's that on your lips, Ronnie?

What?

He wiped the back of his hand across his mouth and looked at the red smear. The cunt. She set him up.

I said I wouldn't tell if he kissed me.

Ronnie. That was Lynda sounding hurt.

He's a wimp.

You tit.

Ronnie!

Well, she is.

Hey, I want one.

Before he could move Nih had kissed him too and stuck her tongue in his mouth. She tasted like cherry lipstick. Her hand grabbed his ass and he was ready to scream he didn't know what the....

Leave him alone.

Your turn, Lynda, lover.

C'mon, Lynda. C'mon. Do something.

Nih pushed Ronnie and Lav pushed Lynda and they came awkwardly together. He could feel her hard belly. Her face wasn't beautiful like the others.

Kiss me, Ronnie.

The other two watched. He could reach out and touch them both. On the thing. On the...pussy. He heard them saying Ronnie's a virgin. Ronnie's scared. He became invisible. They couldn't see him. They didn't exist. Whatever they did didn't exist. The invisible man walked over to the fridge and got another beer and looked right through them. He wasn't there. He wasn't a person. He was a baseball fan but not a person. He couldn't care less about girls. They were invisible. He was invisible. They may have been talking. They may have pulled Lynda's top down. Maybe he kissed her maybe he didn't. There were three pussies in the room. At the back of his mind he knew that. They giggled and drank wine and their bodies were everywhere. All over the room. But they might as well have been ads on TV. He switched channels. One of them maybe sat by him, put his arm around her. Maybe one of them was crying. He switched channels. One might have got sick. One might have watched the game. One might have tried to reach between his legs. He switched channels. One of them might have said she loved him. He switched channels. He might have kissed one of them. It didn't matter. It wasn't him. He was invisible.

I love you, Ronnie.

He swallowed the beer. He watched Devo. He switched channels. Cool man, the invisible man. Can't look down, can't pay attention. Yr a fool goddam goddam goddam fool, goddam goddam girls. Switch channel channel channel channel. One of them might have might have might have. Ronnie the robot cool man cool down switchin and gone outa sight of all that stuff that terrible stuff, single to right by Joe Carter right on man.

Now and Then, A Drinker in Love

It was a half-lit restaurant, very tasteful, very expensive, a shade wrong for reading but just right for conversation in low tones, for business or romance, unless you were with Burgess who specialized, on select occasions, in loudness. He selected them. And he was most loud and most alive only when he was drinking, and the only way to keep up to him was drink for drink all the night long. First it inures you to shame and then encourages you to assume, with Burgess, that all the quiet people looking askance at your table were dead from the neck up, or the neck down, it didn't matter which, for you are the chosen.

I don't know why they let the suburbs into this downtown café, said Burgess, attacking the pastel decor, having just completed a memoir of recent escapades and his monologue on taxation as the contemporary form of pain and penance and therefore much to be desired.

It feels like we're eating inside a giant hollow peach.

No, Michael said, it's like being inside an architect's wet dream.

The plants are eating all our goddam oxygen, said Burgess, butting his cigarette in the nearest offender. Take them out and see if they can live in nature like the rest of us.

Our waitress, whose jet black hair needed a spray job to match the place, poured coffee and turned the handles for our convenience.

But I'm left-handed, said Burgess. Honey I'm left-handed.

I'm sure you'll figure it out, sir. You seem very intelligent.

Join us for a drink, you clever thing.

She turned him down for the fourth time. The decor was actually a muted green and a muted peach, like an unripe cantaloupe. I quit listening and let my mind go on idle and it spent time on the extraordinary comfort of caves like this given the amount of discomfort, deprivation, desperation out of doors. You can range whole systems of belief against each other on the basis of an evening like this. The costumes of the waitresses did match the wallpaper and the plates did echo the paintings. Burgess had returned to the gross bungling of those nameless bureaucrats and politicians he named who had demanded after repeated refusals that he file an income tax return even though for years he had always found so many expenses to deduct – do let me take the collection for this meal and I'll pay – so many business losses and so much depreciation that he'd never paid the grit and tory bastards a blue cent.

That is a measure of how virtuous a man I am. I am not responsible for....

Would you like more coffee, sir?

What? Yes.

Was it regular?

You have irregular coffee?

You seem to have learned to drink right-handed, sir.

Oh do join us for a drink?

We kept the kettle of conversation boiling. Carson took his turn by telling jokes.

What kind of bee gives milk?

What kind? Pause to let us think. C'mon, what kind?

Boo bees.

Much laughter in spite of ourselves. How many feminists does it take to screw in a light bulb? Pause to let us think. One, and it's not funny. Sarah swears she'll pass it on at the office. How many country and western singers to screw in a light bulb? One, and three to make up a song about the old one. In time the place emptied and we, pushing back our chairs and leaning back expansively, cigars flourishing – is that why everyone left? – Burgess accusing Michael of smoking his penis, brandy being snifted and muzzling our brains, for a day at least, the evening an excellent prognostication for the profitability of the Aspirin industry.

Have you tried Vitamin B Complex? Myelinates the nerve ends. Keeps you from dying the morning after. Well, the first morning after.

I take antihistamines cause they can keep you asleep and then dozy. They don't cure a hangover, but at least you aren't awake for all of it.

I just keep on drinking.

Hair a the dog.

No, beer mostly.

You would Burgess, you bloody alky.

You sweet-talking devil.

Booze makes me horny.

It's about time.

Ah, Sarah, don't tell.

And for your hangovers, Sarah?

I don't drink the night before.

Virtue. The refuge of the sober.

I do make a beer special for Michael and I'll make one for all of you tomorrow morning. Beer, clamato juice, salt and everything you can throw in, though he likes radishes best and mushrooms worst. Want one guys?

Oh God.

Absolutely, said Burgess, and a raw egg?

Of course. Basic to the recipe.

Burgess the egg sucker.

Douglas, what was that pale fish you had? The one without any life? Whatsoever.

Cod, poached.

Mild mannered cod, the Clark Kent of fish.

Like everyone else here tonight, said Carson, poached.

That's what happens to whomsoever lives in the suburbs.

I live in the suburbs, said Sarah.

Present company excepted.

I live in the suburbs, said Michael, and I had calamari.

Pretentions above your station.

Can we go now, I'm tired.

One more round, Sarah, one more round.

No, no, no.

Honey! honey! He called the waitress. Five brandies toot de sweet.

I wanted to say no, I've had enough. I'd had enough for a month. But I couldn't open my mouth except to drink whatever came my way. The code of the drinker.

Live for today, said Burgess.

Olé.

Cheers.

Here's to right now.

Everytime you put the glass to your lips it's now, out on the night waves, out on the edge. Liquor makes you think of just where you are. Not of life as an annuity or a pension plan or a stairway to the stars but the next step, the next bun mote in the conversation. Keep the kettle boiling, the drinker's creed. Make it now. Yeah I'll have another drink. And another. What of the hangover? That's tomorrow. A petty pace. You worry about tomorrow, you die today. Who the hell wants to be bourgeois. How many stories can an ordinary guy live? Alcohol's one. Adultery's another. Live your stories where you can.

Six hours. And then Michael drove us home, or started to. When we got to the light at 11th Sarah grabbed the keys out of the ignition and told her husband to change places. He looked at her but saw nothing. He'd lost the power to focus. He started to say no but couldn't remember the word. Burgess climbed out of the back seat, opened the driver's door, ushered him round to the passenger's seat, belted him in and Sarah drove us all home to their place, three guests bunking in and the five of us together for the first time in five years and brandied up to prove it. Then Sarah told us she had a surprise for tomorrow. She smiled. I'm sure she smiled.

> I've invited friends for brunch tomorrow. I'm sure you'll like them. Sleep tight.

We were bound to sleep tight, if we slept at all. Carson gave us each a Hismanal and two Aspirins and a glass of water. But now we were all Michael, speechless, appalled, drunk beyond repair, with a champagne and orange juice, quiche and conversation, brunch tomorrow with neighbours we'd never met before who would be cold sober and decent, well-to-do and expensively casual, in total charge of their own little worlds, with the assurance that comes with voting tory, God help us. Hell in the suburbs. This was after all Metrovia where the gas lawnmower was king and backyards were surrounded by eight-foot-high stained cedar stockades, or unstained among families of taste. Let nature take its course. Which of course it had tonight and would again tomorrow. And so of course morning arrived.

Wakey, wakey, wakey.

Jesus, Burgess.

I stuck my head under the pillow. He left. I lay there. I felt lethargic. That was too positive a word. I was without energy. I was without will. I was too tired to deal a hand of solitaire or pour a glass of water. Stewing in my own juices. I was being acted upon by my own committment to pleasure, my own need to live for the moment, to gather all of life up into one ball, one drink, the last drink – or the last but one – on the edge of the present. Because if we didn't who would. Keep the kettle boiling. The fanatics of pleasure. Who thought restraint betrayal.

Then the water hit my face. Which came to life briefly.

Jesus, Burgess.

But he'd gone on to other challenges of rebirth. It's hard to like a man who doesn't share your hangover. I got up because I had to piss. Walked into the shower and turned it cold and let it go. Threw up in the can. Had another Hismanal, four Aspirins and a vitamin B. Climbed the stairs. Sarah had terrorized Michael into setting the picnic table under the apple tree under the cirrus clouds under the blue tent of the sky. Ah, it was a beautiful day. Unhungover birds sang. Flowers that never touched a drop nodded brightly. The mowed lawn was submissive and green. Carson appeared, bless him, feeling as shitty as I did, swore a red streak at the insensitive Burgess, who actually bragged about his poached-cod, mild-mannered hangover. A sonuvabitch sans doubt. Cheerfully helping Sarah in the kitchen.

I'll pick a bouquet for the table. Here, let me

open the pickles. What a lovely bowl for fruit.

What a smarmy bastard, and we could barely keep our coffee down.

Sarah, that's a lovely summer dress, lovely silk,
goes with your hair, sweetie.

I threw up in the john again, swallowed cold water, took a hot-as-hot-tar crap as the liquor made its vile exit in all directions, irrigated my backside. Such a local pain was a pleasure in a way, however sharp. It could be brought under control and so helped obscure the dull nag of death that now worked overtime within me. Look on the bright side.

Sarah, I think we'll sit Douglas between Martha
and Jeannette. What do you think?

I'll kill him. If you sit with guys they forget your pecadillos. They've been there before. But women are bored with your stupidity, never having ventured out to the last moment with you nor ever will, being the intuitive race, too limited by instinct to ever follow you to that philosophical commitment to the now expressed late at night in the deepest recesses of the male mind by whatever abstraction tickles your logic. The fanatics of pleasure. So there.

They arrived, a quartet, casually expensive, one or two shades older than ourselves but looking younger, days in the facial moistener, at the hair stylist, members of both sexes. Martin was a professor of ontology or oncology or the occult. George was an orthodontist for the oil industry and did some sort of highly specialized drilling and brace work. Martin was English and George American and in their various ways they destroyed the Canadian language. Past became pahst and paast. Canada became Canader or up here. The women, Martha and Jeannette, who belonged respectively, respectably, to etc. and etc., sounded Canadian and under interrogation confessed the same, one from Hamilton, a shade American in the eh, and one from Nova Scotia, a lovely music in the voice, like a deep-throated bird. I fell in love in a minute and a half.

The men told stories of business and government in Metrovia and Carson said they were very amusing and Michael and Sarah laughed. Burgess bustled about like the hired help. The brunch went on for hours. The orange juice was wonderful. It kept raining on my parched throat. Sometimes it had bubbly wine in it. Sometimes Carson told of his days as a hockey player in junior tier B because Martha seemed interested in athletes of the opposite gender. He was the kind of guy who used to open beer bottles with his teeth in the days before the screw top made his folk skills obsolete.

> So anyway the Cougar defencemen wanted my head yknow and I was going down the left wing like a bat outa and he took aim like I was a prairie chicken and he was – did I tell you? – he was twice as big as me – I was 158 in those days soaking wet – I was in real good shape – but he was big, but stupid, big but stupid, and he decided to board me ass end first, ass over tea kettle, but I went into overdrive and squeezed through and he smashed into the boards and got five minutes for deliberately trying to injure his own ass. Butt end Wilson

we called him. So what I did next....

Carson could go on forever. One out of ten stories was mildly interesting unless you were an oldtimers hockey player or you found male athletes interesting, or ex athletes who'd spun lady tales an entire lifetime. His specialty he always said in the bar was the broad jump. Why the hell did we keep him as a friend? And invite him to drinking class reunions? I guess because he'd been there all those years. Because he never dared tell hockey stories to us. Because his marriage broke up and he was on his own. Because he was good natured. Because he was a disciple, both of Burgess and myself. He made us feel larger. How can you know you're great unless someone says you are? Michael and Sarah put up with us, liked us, tolerated us, enjoyed us, but they had each other. Our trio was on the downside of partnerships or marriage. Eight other members of the drinking class of '63 hadn't made it at all. Carson was important to us.

And I was in love. Nova Scotia Jeannette was slight in build, late forties, a boyish hair cut and a small plain radiant face. My hangover focused entirely on that face, especially when it smiled. The last half of every hangover always made it clear to me that I was born on the horns of a dilemma. Oh I never expected anything to come of all my passions. The wild desire was usually sufficient, to be an animal which desired, adored, longed for, without an ounce of good sense or caution or temporizing. I had many marvelous love affairs in my mind, on the furthest reaches of the possible, and bits and pieces in the real world. One roaring marriage for a few years before it turned black. Now she was beside me, not a face in the crowd, nor a paper lady in fiction or photography. But in the flesh, a small bundle of flesh covered in translucent skin of the rose and peach variety. Was it makeup or was it reality? Covered in a silk dress that swelled to the two-hand size at the hips.

She ran a gallery. We talked of painters. I asked prices, expressed surprise at what was worth four thousand and what you could pick up for a song at four hundred. We admired Gravel, Perrault, Sinclair, MacDonald, Olito. We talked of each painter, of ten others, repeated our admirations two or three times. It was delightful to have a topic of such mutual and deep interest. We accepted in turn wine, cheese, sunshine, sweet air, waved away wasps and kept talking, graciously acknowledging at intervals the presence of others.

Her husband George talked of his hobby, his family tree, that spread from Texas to the eastern seaboard and all the way back to the old country. It had many branches. Carson was, believe it or not, an historian who had written books that someone had published, notably one on the hegemony of money over damn near everything on the Canadian frontiers. There were five frontiers I believe from east to west to north and then to now. The oilidontist said oh yes and continued to talk of each leaf on the tree and when and how he'd plucked it. Burgess said later well he can't write poor fellow so he has to tell it over and over. It's his form of publication poor dear. Burgess listened attentively, as nice to the storyteller as he had been to the waitress. A collector of stray cats.

Have you ever travelled the inland passage, Jen?

No I haven't but I've always wanted to.

It's lovely. You just sit there indoors or out, and it all just comes to you, scenery after scenery. You don't have to do anything.

Like now.

Just like now. Jen. Just like now.

Everytime I said her name my heart pumped more blood.

Who did you travel with?

With God. God's own scenery. Nothing more beautiful, Jen. Than the inland passage travelled together.

I will have another glass. Thanks, William.

His name's Burgess. Call him Burgess or he'll turn into a head waiter forever.

Can I fill you up, Douglas? You sweet-tongued devil you.

You're a real sweetheart, Burgess.

I hope I didn't interrupt anything, he said in my ear, and smiled like a two-hundred-pound cherub.

I was just planning my future.

Live for the moment, Dougie boy.

From moment to moment I lived that afternoon, like a drinker in love, and every minute was lovely, her smiling, her speaking with that clear voice like she'd distilled summertime in her vocal cords, but now there was suddenly the future, not only the very precise future of possible sexual penetration or engulfment, but that other one too, the frightening one, of talking for years to the same person, looking at the same thing, driving in the same car, constructing the same memories of a shared past. As if the present were unimportant, a way station on a long journey. That was a very disturbing thought to a drinking man, to a fanatic of pleasure, to a once-hurt-twice-shy guy.

Are you feeling all right, Douglas?

I was thinking.

Are you okay?

It doesn't hurt that much.

I didn't mean... And she laughed.

My hangover is now in retreat, except for the residue of animal passion for members of the opposite sex.

I should drink more, she said.

You've done just fine this afternoon.

I have, haven't I?

And any drinker would be proud to escort you to a mixed bar.

Finally it was lean back, stretch, coffee time. I turned down the brandy. I turned down the Cointreau. Jen had a Cointreau. I had water. I had to think of tomorrow. I had a future to consider. I had a love to declare in clear and blatant terms. Like, I love you. I'd said that already but not in so few words. Was it serious for her when it was life and death to me? A parched hungover life looking for morning, for summer. Jesus, the desire was on the rise again and I had to play the line out slowly in the cool mountain stream hoping like hell that I would be the lure and the stream and the fish and she'd reel me in or dive in or whatever. Reel me in, darling, I'm dying on this gravel shore. Drag me into deep water.

Burgess declared his love for George and asked to marry him. No response, said Burgess, but we're lunching on Tuesday where I'm to give advice about, and hope to climb, the family tree. And then there's tax evasion. He's fascinated with tax evasion.

Next day I invited Jen for lunch at the Corral. I saw it all before it happened. An isolated booth. White tablecloth. Silver silver flashing in the dim light. A beverage over which one might or might not say everything. I had already decided to adore her. A $60 lunch, with wine. That's a serious commitment. And the present will dissolve in the oils of love and liquor and we will live like others, now, then and forever.

The meal would be served. We would exchange small talk. I would declare my love. Let me drink your lips, I would say, and feast upon the slender elegant fields of your body. Fields often harvested and still this year golden with new growth. Or words to that effect. Over I think a martini. Or a bloody gomez. Or a scotch and soda. Darling, I would say, you're beautiful, cool and fluted like a glass of chablis. Will you love me through all the courses of dinner? From aperitif to the final brandy, death closing the door at last on all your crystal and silver. I do so look forward to all we will have shared.

A drinker in love and sinking into the future for the third time.

Joni Went to Market

Lean sky and the anorexic prairie.
Highway unwinding its movie without beginning or end.

Larry. Larry!

Jesus, I told her a thousand times. Don't interrupt me when I'm writing.

Larry! Please.

Can't hear a thing. There's a bird in a tree. The low surf of traffic. The anorexic prairie.

Larry.

It's a delicate balance knowing how long you can hold out before it's more trouble holding out than giving in.

Damital Larry!

If she gets mad enough we have to fight. Silence. Long silence. Can't write a damned thing now. She's in my mind. Why'd she quit calling? Did she reach the sugar herself? Carry the vacuum cleaner upstairs herself? Can't write. Might as well get a drink. This July heat is murder. Taste of salty sweat. House is bloody dark. Blink out all that sun. Maybe I'll have a game of solitaire till my mind clears itself out. Where the hell is she? Not in the kitchen. Living room.

Delores.

Silence. Where the hell's she gone? Bedroom. Everything's in place but her. Upstairs. No, no, can't walk upstairs. Look like I'm looking.

Delores, you up there?

Nothing. What's she up to? Playing games? Car's still out front. Should I try the basement. Maybe she's hurt. Better check.

Delores? You down there?

Silence. Black feeling in my stomach again, like I've had too much coffee. Okay, okay, I'll look in the closet, check if her clothes are there. Well I'll be a....

What the hell are you doing in the bloody closet?

There she is sitting quietly in the corner under all her blouses as if she were just spending another day in the closet. In the closet!

What are you doing in there for Chrissakes!

Hiding.

Hiding?

What the hell for?

For the hell of it.

I've told her a thousand times I make the word plays around here. I'm the poet.

You miss me? she asks.

What?

When you couldn't find me anywhere. Did you

miss me?

Don't be stupid.

You went all over the house looking.

I was looking for a deck of cards.

And then you looked in my closet.

Yeah.

So why look in my closet?

If you can't say anything real mean don't say anything at all.

We've never kept the cards in here.

Go ahead honey rub it in.

Can't say it? she asks.

Last time I said something nice we had twins.

Look, why don't you come outa there. Must be hot as Hades in there. Come on, I'll give you a hand.

The hand of compromise. Try the magic word.

Please. Delores.

I like it in here.

You must be baking. It's like an oven in this place.

I'd like a drink.

You'd like a drink? In there?

Yes.

Okay, I can arrange that.

Sometimes you gotta humour them. It's what you get for marrying a woman. Though there aren't many options. Okay, the tequila, the tonic, the lemon juice, the Nanton water, the large glass, the ice. No ice. Nobody's perfect.

Where's my drink?

I'm breaking the ice, I shout.

Well, so to speak.

Hurry up, I'm thirsty.

Give em an inch. Where the hell's the jigger. Doesn't matter. Captain's measure. Carry in two glasses, give her one, sitting in the corner of the bloody closet. Keep the big one for myself. I'm under a lot of strain.

Weird.

Come on in.

Uh, no thanks, I'm hot enough as it is out here.

Don't be a stick-in-the-mud.

Can't think of the last time I heard that expression. She kicks off her shoes. I drink. She drinks. I drink. She drinks. Hot days have one advantage. A thirst that would make a camel proud.

Well, drink up honey.

That's part of an old joke between us so I can use the word without committing myself. Irony is a wonderful glue. It sticks but it doesn't bind.

You want another?

Sure.

In there?

Mmm hmmm.

I go get two more. Captain's measure. Turn on the radio and get told to buy a hamburger, a car and to go to a movie about poltergeists whatever the hell they are. I kill that junk and spin a disk. That's my era. So. Hot day cool jazz. Miles Davis *Kinda Blue.* Listen to that music. The cool blue waves arriving on shore at regular intervals.

Where's my drink?

Getting a bit insistent she is.

Tequila coming in.

She's unbuttoned the top two buttons on her blouse.

Hot enough for you?

Come on in, the water's fine.

Delores what the hell are you doing in the bloody closet? Am I gonna have to phone a doctor about you? Do I have to bring you your meals in there? You gonna come out to go to the bathroom?

What were you looking in my closet for?

Oh, we're back to that again are we? And what did you want when you called me?

I called you?

Silence. Tricked. Bone stupid.

You mean you heard?

Drink drink. That's one drink for each of us.

How many times did I call?

I heard once.

Oh.

Back she goes into the corner, into her steam bath.

You like Miles? I ask, as a diversion.

You put that on for me?

Uh. Yeah.

I'd like Joni Mitchell.

Okay, when the record's over.

Now.

Shrug. This is a thing I never argue about. I've spent thousands of dollars on records and a machine to play them on. When I get a request I fill it. Then I can buy another record and not feel guilty. What'll I pick? *Black*

Crow I like. Travelling and highways and flying like that crow in the blue sky. Good hangover record. Ice cool voice. Stretched back face. Woman on the road. My woman in the bloody closet.

Well, there's Joni.

Only where the hell's Delores? The cupboard is bare.

Delores! Where the hell are you this time? In the oven? Jesus Christ, woman!

I'll be damned if I'm gonna look for her again. Kids'll be home soon. That'll straighten her out. I'll top up this drink. Upstairs. Under the bed. Study. My closet. Car's there. In your lady's chamber. God, it's hot. Where the hell is she? Ready or not here I come. Home free. Once in awhile. Basement. No, she wouldn't be there. Too cool and comfortable down there. Sensible. Probably did climb in the oven and turn on the time bake. Nope.

Delores.

Silence.

Delores! Damital, Delores!

I'll keep my eye on the bar. Catch her when she comes back for a refill. Too damn hot. Maybe there's a breeze outside. Back to the patio. In this heat we'll all melt and turn anorexic. Well I'll be a....

What are you doin out here? Goddarn it woman.

Having a drink. It's nice out here. And you brought me a refill. Thanks.

I give her my drink. Plenty where that came from. Now she's wearing a peasant skirt. Halter. My ball cap perched on the back of her head.

Why don't you get yourself a refill?

Will you stay put?

Maybe.

You like Joni?

Thank you.

Back down I go to the magic bar and put together takillya and mixins. Whistle it together. She's a helluva hot day. Oh oh. Out the corner of my eye. I see her. I see her. Sneaking back to the bedroom but she can't fool me. Come out of the closet, honey.

Howdy.

Oh.

Don't go into the closet again, please.

Cheers.

Cheers, I reply. You look kinda, uh, kinda....

It's the gesture that counts.

How many times did I call you? she asks.

I don't know. I don't remember.

Guess.

Well, five.

Why did you look in the closet?

I was afraid you'd left.

In tequillam veritas.

Why would I ever leave you?

Oh oh. Trick question. Land mines all around that one. Cut her off at the pass or we'll waste all this good liquor. Truth is okay but you can overdo it.

Can't imagine. What did you want me for?

Can't remember.

I'm sorry I didn't reply. I was working.

An apology. Think of that. Well, sort of an apology. More'n

usual. I hold out my glass and we clink. Then she lifts her peasant skirt. And she is a peasant. Making the summer summer. I drop my pen. Anorexia be damned. The prairie is a sandwich, white bread clouds, brown bread fields. We're the filling. Joni went to market and we stayed home.

Car Thing

I. Car Thing

Get out of bed early, the sun already up, warming the garden. Go out on the deck with my coffee. Smell that air. More clean air than people here in Canada, not like London, poisoned air all summer long, stinking cars breathing out high tar. Nobody's around in the alley, oh, there's one of the condo girls, the tall girl, a bit ungainly, great smile, like now, hi, wave wave. I like that girl, half-time advertising, ex-art student, found her cat for her once, she should lose it again, that's life on the edge. Great day to walk the dog if there was one. What's wrong with her car? Got a cough. Can't go on the road with that. My ex gone down the road, gotta kill time somehow. Her car's going terminal, gone dead. I'll be the good mechanic and lift her hood.

Hey, you need a hand?

Can't get a peep out of it.

Here let me try.

Climb the fence, turn the key. It's just mumbling, it's got a hangover.

Your car's got a hangover.

Shit, I've got a client in 20 minutes.

Lift that hood, smell that engine, that good dirty oil smell in the morning.

Battery's corroded.

It was perfect yesterday.

I'll put my shoes and shirt on and be your chauffeur.

She says I don't have to go to that trouble, can I pay you, I say of course not, stick my feet in loafers, drop on a T-shirt that says Clear Cut and shows a giant lawnmower eating downtown Vancouver. She gets in my old Cavalier, I dump my crap in the back.

You're the navigator.

It's the AECL building on 2nd.

You advertising nuclear?

I'm doing a pamphlet.

You wear lead pants?

It is only an office.

Turn over the bridge to downtown, about as much traffic in the entire city as on one road in London.

This is really kind of you. I'm Jan.

I've decided this is my day for good deeds. I'm Lefty.

There it is.

You know what's funny about that building? The

domed skylights look like mushroom clouds.

Gosh, you're right. Should I tell them?

Up to you, Jan.

Gotta go. How can I thank you?

You owe me one.

Gone, into corporate Canada, dark glass door closing. The sun's out, sidewalk warming. For Cavalier air conditioning roll down the window by hand, none of these fancy buttons, picking up speed, commencing to pick up speed, what the fuck put some distance between myself and myself. Or go home and climb in the shower. I hate these decisions. Just how did the corporate testicles spread out over the land? And in the air. Amazing there is any air at all with all the faxes flying about, low level angels. The pure invisible technology of Angel Fax.

Stick my hand into the dirt, pulling weeds in the carrots. Half a row and straighten up, my back sore as hell, stretch in the sun, not enough wet to find a worm, lived like a worm in that basement London flat, rain dripping day after day. Climbed out to the street, worm of the day, black worm, black pants, black shirt, and a black brolly, like a smoker's lung out for a bit of air. Night all day long at Bayswater. Okay, tomatoes, time to pick off the suckers in this giant lake of sun, beautiful tomato scent. Gotta stretch and there's girl two off to work, climbing in her Honda, big-assed girl, short and thick, maybe her car won't work and I can check under her hood. Jesus Christ, it won't start, got some terrible disease.

Can you help me, sir?

Sir, that's me. Sir. What a fuck to be older, every day it's the same thing, playing death one day at a time, but 38 ain't so bad. So what if she's in her first bra. And a titter ran through the crowd. Won't leap the fence this time. It hurt. Put my shirt back on, Canadian formal. The tail that wagged the girl.

What's wrong?

Won't turn over.

Sounds like it's got the flu.

Lift the hood. Fucked battery.

Battery gone. It's pneumonia.

What the fuck's goin on? Sokay yesterday and Jan's car wouldn't start either. So what the fuck.

What's your name?

What the fuck does that matter?

Hey, take it easy, you invited me over. Remember? Sir?

Penelope.

No wonder you don't want to tell people your name.

You don't like it, piss off.

Penny for your thoughts.

You and every other jerk. You gimme a ride like you did for Jan?

Absolutely, Pen, and where are you going this morning?

Golden Horseshoe on 22nd.

Leave to wash the garden off me. She wears it tight, tight ass jeans in this weather, tight T-shirt. Always know where her legs are meeting.

Climb in, Pen.

What's yr name?

Len. Len n Pen eh? Sounds good.

You're one a them. I meet you all the time.

You do volunteer work at an old age home?

Over the bridge into the blue sky. We're on an eight-light trip this time.

Just how old are ya, Sir?

Where's the Golden Horses whatever?

Shoe. It's country and western. I'm a waitress for lunch. Gotta set up and then I get the afternoon off and do the nights. It's half dance floor, and it's wild at night and sometimes good tips eh and that's why I dress like this. I seen you watching my ass.

The tail that wagged the girl.

You look in my window?

Whenever I get the chance Pen. You got nice pink shower curtains.

How old are ya?

Old enough to be your father, if I married at 16. You like older men?

There's the old Horseshoe.

Looks a bit shabby.

Lotta assholes get really drunk and stupid. We fix it and they trash it. We're okay causa these big fuckin bouncers like Walter.

Bye Pen.

Penelope.

Lenin.

What kinda name's that?

I'm named after the great Russian Communist leader. My parents were socialists.

Parents can sure fuck ya up. Or are you just fulla shit?

That too.

Hey can you dance?

One step at a time.

You got a dance whenever you want one. Like for the ride.

Sir.

Yeah, sir. See ya.

I'm in love, Pen.

Oh yeah who with?

Gone, gone, into the half-life of the Golden Horseshoe, foreign country, seen those dance steps on TV, you need to be a genius. Golden Horseshoe Special, Wrangler's Pasta, $6.95, Starring Tonight, Cass McRobbie and her Laredo Chums, Dancing till the Cows Come Home. I'd sure as hell six beers down give a tip to horny Penelope. Gotta head out, gotta drive, ride out of the memories, love lost / I'm hidin she's ridin / one house and one car / I'm at the table she's in the Sable / I'm hiding she's ridin / for all she's worth / my fingers in the earth / she's on the highway, freeway, goin always new days. What a writer, what a writer. Doesn't do any good, wishful thinking as always, keep the spirits up, and whatever else, that Pen that Pen and don't think about it, I saw that Ford half-ton before.

Washing down the Cav, nice in the heat to hose a car dripping from head to toe. Spic and span hub caps. Cav ain't no hell but it's best to look your best, sun hot on my back, enough sun and you get younger, the sunshine fountain of youth, Cav so full of handsome women it's your best day old Cav even if you look as bad as I do. But cars can get shined up, look better than people, I take it back here comes the owner of the fancy van. Is she older than me? Enough makeup to sink a rowboat, she's simonized her face. Enough cleavage to make Lazarus rise from the bed. This is July and she's dressed for the onslaught of winter. Hot hotter hottest, upholstered on the bottom, brocaded on the top, scared of her body and who isn't. Me in the sun washing the car to make my life more clean, fuck London, fuck ex, more shiny, more orderly. To hell with time, old images, old car, old garden like mom's, old body I had all my life, new sun, new day, Jesus her car's fucked too and I get to climb under her hood brocade and all.

You need some help, lady?

Oh I do, yes I do. Machines just terrify me. Thank you, thank you.

Me under her hood smelling that lovely engine.

Your car's got a disease.

Oh my.

Carbonitis.

Oh my.

And it's fucked besides, you'll need a tow.

Oh my goodness.

Want a lift? Norm's taxi service for distressed females.

Really, will you really?

Come on, hop over the fence.

Perhaps the long way round would be more decorous. And I'm Ethel, honey.

More decorous, yeah, you are, indeed. Open the door and she gingerly sits down with her kit bag beside her.

I cleaned the outside, working my way in. Where to?

Well I am embarrassed really, but it's the fitness centre on 52nd.

Working out eh? Lose a few pounds. Get into fighting shape.

Well, something like that, yes.

If you scraped the paint off your face you'd lose a pound right there.

Good heavens.

You're a good lookin woman, Ethel, so why hide it behind the gup. You got powder on your bosoms too. Wanta go to the movies tonight? Jackie Chan in the Bronx. Lotsa action. He does his own stunts yknow. Lotsa humour. Like a good relationship, action and a few laughs. Whataya think?

It's just ahead.

Oh the body shop, no the upholstery shop, ah, no the Weigh Out.

Thank you for the ride.

Pick you up at six-thirty for the movie.

Oh my.

She's gone gone, inside, only one condo babe left, down the window, nature's air conditioning. Day's gonna boil right over. Comes to the movie, doesn't come to the movie, ready to boil over, me ready to boil over, head for the highway leave it all behind.

What a difference a day makes and why's that Ford half-ton still around, lots of Ford half-tons, relax, must be a hundred of them in town, I haven't talked to so many dolls in one day since I was a teacher's aide. Out of practice. Talk to em once and never see em again, that's my speed. Except the ex. God, thousands of sentences. She talked more than she smoked. London's a big city, she could occupy it with her mouth alone. Sometimes I think there might even be something wrong with me. Gotta gas up at Petrocan. Do it yourself. Who needs employees? Bunny rabbit for a cashier. Soft eyes that'll eat you alive. Takes my credit card, there's that Ford half-ton getting gas getting on my nerves. I'll do the quick right, up the alley, out on the crescent, hate those trees with the bands on them, like they're wearing garter belts, back into a driveway behind the hedge and by God there he goes. He ain't my idea of a tail job, kinda exciting anyhow, pick up the day, Ford pickup of the day. My idea of a tail job is that painted Ethel or big Pen, covered all over with nothing but words, my words, sweet violets, all over, I oughta be an artist. Okay, that Ford is history, I'll go the long way round, maybe he knows my house anyway, what the hell, a little excitement with nothing to do all day but garden, drive beautiful women to their destinations, write my memoirs, pass time. I can go to the bar when the shadow of the car is bigger than the car, but it's hard to wait, could die of thirst. Slip into my back alley with the giant green stupid garbage containers and there's that tiny girl going out to her old bug, son-of-a-bitch, Volkswagon's got the same disease, a little cough, a sputter or two, car plague must be catching, an automobile epidemic, the pox, carbonitis, motor mouth, smokin too much, can't stand their own exhaust, the only good car's a dead car.

Hi. Hi! Hello!

She's occupied or her ears are as small as her bod. Climb the fence, drop down on the grass, just call me Jackie Chan. Hello, try it again, Christ, got her head under her own hood.

Car gone dead eh?

Why are they all still here? I'm always the last to leave.

All gone dead.

My battery's gone. Can you help?

A car is a complete mystery to me but I can give you a lift. Mine is disease-free this morning.

I don't want to impose. And I wouldn't do this but I'm late for class.

She's so tiny she's like a miniature woman.

You should bike.

I love cars, just love being in a car, driving, I love driving.

I'm Lenin.

I'm Norylayne.

Where to?

Arts Building.

Whatcha taking?

Sociology.

Gee, a nice girl like you.

And Women's and Gender Studies.

I knew a Jan.

Pardon.

Stopped at a light, waiting for the only two cars on Clarence to go by. Fit the whole city into a corner of London, except the women here, Jesus, fresh as the day is long.

Jan, short for Jander, she lives in the bottom flat. But you're not studying her right? And how come you like driving if you only got a bug?

My dad left it to me in his will.

Sorry. Was he vertically challenged?

Well he loomed large in my life.

You like father figures?

You're not quite old enough and I get out here.

Say hello to Jan for me.

Come to class one day, we could teach you the real world.

II. The Detective of Rumours

Carver didn't understand why they'd hired him. He'd put his name in the classifieds, Carver F, private investigator. It was a last resort. Jazz piano was every second weekend now and going nowhere, the halcyon days of tours in the mid and far west a memory. His fingers were nimble as ever, his mind alive at the keyboard and nowhere else. A light-fingered piano player following in the fingerprints of Hampton Hawes. Unlocking the doors to the cool Pacific and days both blue and quiet. Confidentially Guaranteed. A private eye, a private tongue. He proved he was private whenever he was hired. He always said as little as possible, as if he were being interrogated. Fee quietly agreed on. Received photos and was on his way, tracing a guy who hadn't paid on his car, following a woman who was suspected of loving two men at the same time. Boring stuff. Hours in his old half-ton waiting, reading the newspaper, a detective story, music magazines. Watch and wait. That was the game. Passing time, but he often thought it was time passing him.

Now he was hired to follow rumours.

He'd met the fellow in a hotel room that looked like every other hotel room. There was an assembly line of hotel rooms made in Detroit or Dallas.

> We're interested in someone who'll keep his mouth shut.

Carver didn't reply.

> And his ears open.

Carver dropped his face into neutral. He practiced in front of a mirror. To make a face no one could read.

> And knows how to be invisible.

Carver was 54, in slacks and a denim shirt, with a face that looked tired, a bit droopy, glasses. He was harmless looking, always a bit absent, as if he was paying attention to something inside himself.

> You are a detective?

Carver nodded. The man with the soft face and the deep voice gave him money and 20 pages of addresses.

Contact me.

How long am I hired?

Carver's voice had no resonance. His life was in his finger tips.

A year. If you find things.

The man left and Carver walked out into the carpeted walls, took the elevator that was playing Ray Connif muzak, walked through the lobby where the employees talked in whispers and stepped into the unruly sun like into a holiday. Drove around town in his air-conditioned Ford half-ton checking all the houses on the printout. Each had the same sign on the door: "This is a Nuclear Free Zone." Carver couldn't understand the sign. He knew a thing or two about uranium, and it didn't stop at doors. Then he thought, is that a rumour? He drove up and down streets, found other signs and added new houses to the list of rumours. Then he'd begun stakeouts. Today he did a stakeout on an old two-storey house. He could stay in the shade of the elms. Out of the radioactive sunlight pouring through holes in the ozone and depleting skin all over the great plains. He turned on a tape of Chico Hamilton, slouched down and waited.

But he wasn't invisible. Not in an old neighbourhood where no one waited in cars for an hour. Mrs. Oleniuk wondered why he was there. Mrs. Anderson wondered why he was there. They phoned each other and spread rumours about him. Was he watching the man next door who watched the girls through his deck trees? What was he up to? Who had he got in trouble? Or was it the artist in the three storey? They never trusted him ever since he moved in twelve years ago. The people he had to his parties, my goodness, one of them came dressed as a tree and they weren't sure if she had clothes on underneath her leaves. They didn't think so. They told everyone. Carver didn't know you could never hide in a backwater.

The guy in the house drove his blue Cavalier out the alley towards the river, with a female occupant. Carver followed them, to AECL, took a picture of the woman, wrote a note in his black pad, followed the guy back home till he started gardening. He felt like a fool. He was a fool, chasing rumours. He hadn't heard a word anyone said. Perhaps a telephone tap, if he knew how to do one. He opened his hand. He clenched his hand. He opened it again. Nothing there. Not a single rumour flying on the wind. The trip to AECL was the closest he'd got. At least a connection. An AECL pamphlet said, "Radioactivity from the earth is natural like water but there are people who won't accept facts and who spread rumours. They spread them against us." Radioactive rumours in the air. Closed his fist. Opened it. Nothing. But his fingers that play clusters of notes. How far do the notes go? Are there stars listening to King Oliver tonight? Or rumours against Cogema? Watch the liquor stores, the man said, at busy times. See who refuses to buy French wine.

Friday he was back in Buddy's again with the trio, scheming freedom like Hampton Hawes. The Chernobyl All Stars playing the nuclear blues. The Cavalier guy was off with another woman, with a nuclear hairdo, like she'd stuck her finger in a light socket. She's short. She wants to be tall. Or is it a disquise and she's a boy. He liked driving even if he was going no place special. Followed them all the way to country and western on the west end of town. Carver was depressed. He hated country and western more than Connif. He hated it worse than his job. He bought a coffee from a Ukrainian drive-in and followed the Cavalier home. He suspected the driver of the Cavalier. There were so many on the road it was good cover. Just like a Ford pickup of some anonymous year.

He sat and waited. This was his 25th stakeout. He stuck his finger into his coffee and hung it out the window. No rumours stuck to it. He was bored with his job. If it was a job. He got paid. It was a job. He decided he should start to manufacture his own rumours. Cigar Lake was still smoking. AECL meant Atomic Energy Cock-up Limited. Let's all walk the Yellow Cake Road. He didn't tell anyone his rumours so they weren't officially rumours. Unless God could read your mind. He could when Carver was a boy. Rumours would appear on religious broadcasts. The illumination on the road to Nagasaki. Sodom and Gomorrah nuked. What knowledge was learned from the tree of knowledge? Man cannot turn knowledge off. All the way to Armageddon and back, like Oedipus, only by automobile. He hated himself. How could he stop his mind. It was all this spare time. The devil's workshop.

He thought he should knock on the guy's door and ask for some Free Nuclear or some Free Zone. Not a cloud between him and the sun except Fordhood, his salvation. Low flying rumour at eight o'clock. Kid walking by with a suburb blaster. There's another woman in the guy's car. It's a sex-free zone. It was hard to follow a car when there were so few cars. Every car stood out. There was no 401, no natural habitat to hide in. Just the bald-headed streets. Going north. Maybe he's a black market cabbie. Or they're all together in a plot to attack their corporate masters. He felt like a fool. Idiot for hire. He turned on his Ranee Lee tape. He felt sanity wash over him. Oliver Jones piano. Now there's a man with twelve fingers. On each hand. The Weigh Out. The woman was big enough to smuggle half a dozen rumours across the border. Got bored with the guy and decided to stake out the woman, parked the car and walked inside. He needed a workout. His back was dying. It spent too much time in his old truck.

Women are all gone, the Ford's gone, it's hottern hotter, what'll I do all afternoon, write my memoirs, choose which woman, okay, Jan's the nicest but no tits like that joke the ex liked to tell about who a guy chooses, the one with the biggest tits. Ain't it the truth. She's old as me but you could fall in there and thrash around for days to get out again. God it's hot out, gotta get outa this sun, I'll grow old in the dark but there's no help for it, salt's in my eyes, lick up my own salt, go inside for a beer, no sun in this house, man, no woman either, sunspots in my eye, walking blind, find the beer blindfolded, eight steps down into the kitchen, empty, she's not here, not here, get horny when it's so bloody hot, body with you all day long, hanging around there just under your head. Imagine a woman leaving me. Imagine a woman living with me. Going down for the third time, between those tits on big Ethel, going down, hand on a beer, last handhold, still afloat, like a hard turd, head above water, sipping a Labatt's Blue the Canadian beer, Dutch treat sold Alomar so Toronto's dead, new home for the ex and her exhibitions, love to hear of bad weather in Toronto, let her suffer snow and sleet and fuckin heat, cool in the basement, dark as a dungeon, sunshine gone and TV the winner, weather channel, there's continued boiling weather on the prairies, raining cats and politicians in TO, she's an aide or something for one of the Harris tweeds, pussy landing on her feet, I want big Ethel, can't stand this dark, the ex and her soap operas, to hell with melanoma, melt this gut on the deck, sweat off the beer and have another one, no Ford pickup, beer goes down with a zzz zzz zzz, pull the panama hat over my eyes, start the memoir later when my mind's clear, oh sun, eye sockets full of red, flooded with red, red ocean, red caves, hot yellows, holidays are great eh great okay are okay are red goin goin yeah goin goin yeah Ethel Ethel.

When Carver entered Weigh Out the big doll was on some Nordic walking machine. This was not the kind of place Carver frequented.

Sir.

Yes. Bicycle.

We have different levels.

Pause.

Have you been here before, Sir?
No.
First time free. It's our August special.
Do you like jazz?
Jazz, sir?

He climbed on the bicycle. He realized he had no gym clothes. Then he realized his lungs had shrunk. Then his knees started to burn. The doll kept on walking. She walked to Dundurn. She was on her way to Hanley. Her breasts kept pace. Her legs were great. Well, they would be if you walked to Hanley every day. His chest was acting like a small drum on four-four time. There were healthophiles everywhere. He hated it. Carver dreamed of old jazz basements where you had to memorize the piano because you couldn't see the keys for smoke, tobacco smoke, pot, the steamy music, not a bicep in sight. He watched the woman. He began to pedal his bike in time with her bottom shifting from side to side. He forgot the pain. His knees had gone somewhere beyond fire. He decided he had ozone in his knees. He was on automatic pilot. This was the world of health. This was a sickness-free zone. This was a death-free zone. Who was the jogger who had died with his Adidas on? He hated the place. It was nothing but rumour, that's it, nothing but rumour, about living forever, like uranium. Did they want positive rumours? He'd write it up. Send it in. Keep the paycheques coming. The woman was indefatigable. She was on her way to Davidson. She looked like an overstuffed Liz Taylor. Working out like Wonder Woman. He had not had a woman, a serious woman, who would stay beyond a night, for ten years. When jazz went bad, women went bad. Went to health spas. Entered muzak marriages. Some private eye. He kept his eye on her privates. If she didn't stop soon Carver knew he would be a health casualty.

III. Smoke Thing

Would you join me in a cigarette?

Oh my no, I'm on the path to health.

Well now these are particularly healthy cigarettes. I've a green thumb. See? Well, anyway, I grow things. You might not believe it but I am serious about growing.

Oh, that's good.

You pedal yourself to Davidson and back every day and I garden indoors. And when my geraniums get aphids I mix tobacco and water and rub it on the leaves and the aphids....

Do they learn to smoke? Or do they get lung cancer.

They get healthy. The aphids die and the plants grow. It's the same with the lungs. Smoke kills the bacteria.

Really?

I've been much healthier since I've been smoking. And I'm more philosophical. Where does the smoke go? Is our life a cigarette? I only smoke Gauloises. They're French. I import them from Edmonton.

Should I should try one do you think?

Carver put two Gauloises in his mouth, lit them with a match from Buddie's Bar, We're the Match for You. They inhaled together. The scent was very strong.

Oh my, that's certainly different, isn't it.

Carver couldn't be with a woman and not smoke. He inhaled smoke as if he were inhaling her into his capillaries and blood stream. Women gave off an aroma. He inhaled it on the street. He inhaled it now and let out smoke. He was on fire.

You're really sure this is low calorie Scotch?

I'm thin as a rake and I drink it every day.

Oh my.

Oh my indeed, honey. Cheers.

Cheers. Do you think I'm on the road to health?

There was a famous study done in Denmark and it divided liquor into units, so one beer, one shot of whiskey, one glass of wine was a unit. And they followed oh, let's say 30,000 people for 20 years and it proved, now it proved the healthiest people had one unit of booze a day, and get this, if you had seven units a day – that's a bottle of wine – you would have the same life expectancy as a teetotaler. Great eh?

Really? Well I'll have another. Catch up for yesterday won't I?

You can walk it off tomorrow.

Oh yes I can.

Take a different highway. You could make it to Lanigan.

Will you work out too?

I would love to honey but I have my own work to do.

The waiter exchanged ashtrays. The smoke rose lazily. The tape machine played the music of the young. He watched her place the cigarette between her red lips. He wanted to be her cigarette. She inhaled. The cigarette rested between her forefinger and her indecent finger at the tumescent angle.

It was forbidden to smoke at AECL. It was bad for your health. Jan's meeting happened. Mr. Cameron explained that a pamphlet should tell children that radiation was as common and as beneficial as water or air, and sometimes, in the form of x-rays or barium enemas, even more beneficial. Radiation, wisely used, kept people alive longer to enjoy that air and water. Jan showed examples of writing for children. "If you don't want the garbage blues you have to clean your room. If you don't want the garbage blues you have to clean your yard and your street. Never smoke. Or you'll breathe garbage air. Oh. Your poor nose. Your poor lungs." She'd drawn pictures of an unhappy nose, a gasping lung, a boy buried under his room, a girl putting out cigarettes with a squirt gun. It was the friendly family image Mr. Cameron wanted. She got the contract for the pamphlet on the medical uses of uranium for distribution in the schools. She could pay her rent for another three months. Something always turned up. She felt good and decided to walk home. She lit up, no smoking ban yet on public streets, and relaxed.

The Golden Horseshoe was filling up. Penelope was on the run. She liked the band, hated the bartender who was always down on her, wanted the drummer to look at her again. She'd rather dance than serve. She took a deep drag and put her cig on the ashtray at the bar. There was another table of assholes calling her honey buns and when one of them grabbed her ass she smacked him hard on the chin with the tray and backed off and Walter the bouncer walked over when one of them was about to get up. Nobody messed with Walter, and she was nice to him and he protected her like he was her father. She hated those kind of guys. She liked that dobro. Made her feel goozey. Wonder if that guy next door wants to take me out. I'll leave the curtain open a peek when I shower. I got nothin to hide. She took another quick drag. He's got a whole house, must have real money, better'n these retards. Bet I could get him, I bet. Smoke came out her nose. She'd practiced that a lot.

Norlayne went to her sociology class. She spoke up twice. She said it was more difficult for women to have a strong sense of identity than men because it was harder for a house to give an identity than a job where there were so many other people. After class she joined her professor for a smoke. The Arts Building was smoke free. They stood in the shade of Fort Film and she offered him a Rothman's. He flicked his lighter in imitation of the sun. She liked cigarettes because they were bad. She liked her prof. He was tall and large and had a black beard. She was always afraid he might light it on fire. They smoked in silence. She watched the small cigarette in his large hand. She thought of herself as that cigarette. He watched her hold her cigarette delicate as a bird in her fingers. He felt large and awkward. She felt small and shy. The wind blew her cigarette smoke into his cigarette smoke.

IV. Rosy Brown

Oh Christ, hot, where am I, back's sore, sweat pouring down, fell asleep on the deck, that's it. I'm a dishrag, can't move, what can I see? There's my knees, red, Jesus, sun red, rosy brown, rosy brown, if only I knew a Rosy Brown I'd fall in love for life, God I gotta lay something, green slats on the deck, feet stuck out there, my feet, see those toes wiggle, I'm alive, I'm alive, sounds, let's see, sounds of some bird, of some traffic a block away, sounds like a river, shoulder moves, another good sign, I'm not a wounded veteran from the second war of the automobiles, conflagrating like the sun, not like London, sun came out, when was it? Wednesday in late May, eyes move side to side, periscope up, through the maples, four cars no women, yes sir, on to my memoirs, bury the ex to hell with foggy London, free to look at random at all ladies, an entire city waiting, soaked in sweat, get up easy now, knee's locked, shit, knee's locked, give it a wiggle, hand behind it and press, stand up you bugger, stand. Stand. Up. Walk. Nothin to it, what a pro, down them steps. This guy can go downhill. Piss time. The pleasure of drinking is the pleasure of pissing. Whatever goes down must go down, goes down, goes down, goes down, goes down, going for a new world record, forgot to count, leave a cleaner place behind, I kidney not. Shower time. Check the mirror. Fascinating subject. Myself. Now there's a body. It is a body. None like it. Try my best angle. Gut suck. Cock like a leftover thumb. Shower yeah. Swssh Swssh Swssh.

Clean as a whistle so I will not give drinking a bad name, put on my black T-shirt with the barbecue and "Turn me on the rotisserie of love," gets a rise sometimes, topic of conversation, helps break the ice, climb into the car, all the cars are still there next door, no women, hey, there's Jan come home.

Hi.

Hi, thanks again for the ride.

You get the job?

Yeah I did. I'm happy.

Great, see you later.

Drive to the Drink Emporium for Happy Hour, which is about eight hours long and have a pint and there's that dark-haired woman with the scary eyes here again, regular as clockwork, with a cigarette in her hand and that damn smile on her face, oh my, drinking a beer with the blonde, oh God that blonde. It just ain't fair she's allowed to walk around free. I like that hair pulled back so hard and her cheekbones so prominent you can see the skull behind the skin. Nice tan. Rosy Brown. Time to say hello. Cigarette leaning in the ash tray. Little prick.

Puff police are going to get you two.

They laugh.

City council's after really bad people.

Think they'll let us still smoke outside?

In your own backyards. If your fence is high enough.

I've always wanted to be a criminal.

City's gonna hire smoke detectors to spy on you.

Want a smoke?

I would if I smoked.

They laugh. They know every word spoken is carnal. God, I'm sure funny. Take pint two back to my table so I can keep an eye on the bar and those TBs, two beauties, I'm happy as possible, considering. An hour of drinking, maybe more, depends on who comes in. Breathe out. Relax man. Oh yeah. Had a hard day driving all these women. Hard, hard day. Look at those two talking, serious, man are they serious, smoking, like punctuation. Either of them could fill an entire lifetime.

I need a smoke in the best way.

Carver entered the Drink Emporium. Paul Desmond on the tape machine. He was waiting for Ethel. To smoke, to drink, to inhale. The Ford half-ton a block away between vans, invisible. Old habits die hard. He saw the guy he'd been following sitting in a corner with a pint of blond beer. He sat at the bar, lit up and watched. In the lap of luxury he'd forgotten about rumours. Though he'd sent in positive reports about health spas and his catalogues on Nuclear Free houses. He swallowed. Ethel entered in maroon shorts and a pink halter with blossoms on it. He inhaled. The guy walked over to two women. Carver kissed Ethel lightly, took out his notebook and wrote brief descriptions of the new suspects. He thought he ought to follow the blonde. She was emitting something other than smoke. He felt a responsibility to his job.

The Girl Next Door

It's not easy being in this room, not easy at all. The room itself is okay, four walls and a ceiling, a firm mattress, no aching back though an ache is there. It's not my room. It's Mr. Hilton's room. Nothing wrong with the room, a chair and a table to write letters at, a window with a view of another building and another building over that, and clouds over that and blue sky on top. Very comfortable, with a television and a shower and a thermostat.

The problem is next door, which is a room just like mine only it's inhabited by the imagined lady. Have you one of those? Do you know what that can mean? The imagined lady in the next bedroom, only she's for real. We've never been this close in a strange city before. Maybe Toronto's not all that strange but it's not home either and at home close don't count. Wives, husbands, friends, children, uncles, cousins, eyes, all over the city.

You can be very close, like a hello kiss or dancing together, playing cards, talking, but you are always in a web of people, a web of eyes like in a dream sequence in an old movie, a web of things to do, of deadlines, of expectations, and you don't want to break things if you can help it. If you can help it.

Sex is like one of those insects with the long tongues that snap out and gobble up another insect, only sex is invisible and it doesn't actually swallow you and make you disappear. But it touches you, gets inside you, mixes you up. It's a very ordinary day, quotidian as the French would say, trying to make something out of nothing. You've been to the office, talking to clients and staff, of both sexes, some of the women extraordinarily beautiful, yet you're at work and they're a few words and nothing else, sometimes quite amusing words, yours and theirs, but quotidian all the way. Then you get home and your wife says Maureen's invited us over for supper and that tongue's all over you. And if the name can do it think of the person herself.

She gave me a kiss at a party once, a private kiss, a real one, in a back hall, after we'd been drinking. It went right through me. Her lips were so warm, wet, active. I felt her ass as the kiss went on and on and thought, what should I feel next, as an adequate response to that kiss? But we heard someone coming so she said bye everyone and went home. It's still in my head. My dilemma is whether to keep her in the next room, permanently, close enough so that I could, if I decided to, but just out of sight, out of touch. Never out of mind. You can decide what she wears each day, every flavour, every nuance, every second skin. That's a pleasure not to be sneezed at.

Her first husband told me in a bar many years ago how fantastic it had been the first time. He didn't know it could be that great. Know what I mean? Etc., etc. Yeah, sure, right, of course, good, sure, yeah yeah yeah. He was now in hell because they were breaking up. She had someone else he said. He hated her. He could remember what it was like and now it wasn't there. He was in the next room so to speak and it drove him crazy, out of his mind and into ten years of medical treatment, perpetual hatred because she was, well, you know, jesus, I never ever, I couldn't believe, she is, god, she is.... Right pal, she is. I'll take your word for it. Now shut your face. At least you had it. And it took him a decade to get over it and the next time he married he married cool, he married an ice cream cone. She was attractive, slender, lovely, appetizing, but she was cool, the kind you dance with and can never get hold of, like dancing with a stick or a ghost or a night gown. They make all the turns you do but at the far end of your arm. Is she actually there you wonder? But he was right to marry cool. He needed a clipped lawn and an automated kitchen. From hot to cool. Out of the frying pan into the refrigerator. You've only one life. Why throw it away on someone else? It's your life, not hers. Only if she's so deep you have to cut her out of you, then there's no way out is there? Can you amputate a heart? He lived with hatred for so long he can't do without it. He doesn't hate her now, and is on tenterhooks with the new cool wife, who can't stand scenes, but the anger is always there, on the edge, ready to spill out. I think that's why he became so dedicated a right winger. He hates the poor, the lazy, goddam etc. The girl next door can be dangerous, like the smoking ads say, for your health.

I don't want you to get the idea she's perfect in any way, not even in looks. But in my life she is the one in the next room, has been for years, maybe since her first husband talked to me. She's the one in my head. I take her with me on trips. She turns up on streets I've never been in before, on airplanes, buses, when I'm sliding off to sleep and there she is. The world and the mind are filled with beautiful women, but she's the one my fancy's been true to. For years and years. She's not perfect but she is perfectly passionate. That kiss is still in me, knocking around in there. I've been faithful to her in my way. My imagination takes many trips but it always comes home to her. That's fidelity, right?

So now she really is next door, curled in a bed or sitting on a chair, and Toronto is outside, all of it, stretching for miles, and full of nothing but strangers, whole neighborhoods where we wouldn't know a soul. It's a test. I either do or do not say anything. I'm assuming she would say yes. That certainly makes the dilemma a more interesting one. If I say hello and she says so do I, then I step over the invisible line and can't come back again. Without a passport to my name I enter a foreign country and learn to speak a new language. If I say hello the other way and she says hello and that's it, knives and spoons conversation, king and queen of the quotidian, then I cross no invisible line, enter no new country, stay home, remain comfortable, true to my wife. And am plagued with a sense of my own timidity, restraint, cowardice. Plagued for years perhaps. Frank Ashurst in *The Apple Tree.* He chose the cool lady and missed forever the apple tree, the singing and the gold. Passion, story, whatever it was, he missed it. But Maureen is resolutely not Ashurst's Megan, poor passionate young Megan. Megan's mother maybe, and no Treasure House of Atreus untapped, unvisited for years. She's had her own royal succession, of husbands, two more, and lovers, some number or other, and for me one kiss. She's been faithful to me in her way, never upsetting the precise disequilibrium in which we stand towards each other. Or fall. A university friend from long ago, friend of the family, professional woman in no uncertain terms. And at the end of all, of all the years and words, touches and goodbye and hello kisses, I shall be her last male confidante. Here's what my life amounted to and I'm so sad she'll say. Here too is my life, I'll say, the summation of my life. Of course we'll be sad. The bloody thing will be all over and there'll be nothing now, as the poet says, but the inescapable lousiness of growing old. Shit. But not yet, not yet. There's still today and all of Toronto and it's May, sunshine, and so on and so on. What's the time? Turn on the hotel TV, community channel keeping you up to date with Canadian content. It is in central Canada 8:30 a.m. One hour till the conference starts up its engines again and drones implacably forward. I don't have to go. I could skip out. From a conference entitled Canadian Book and Periodical Publishing and the American Presence. I made a speech yesterday at the first general session on the name of the conference itself. I said why would we use, and thus consolidate, the word American, the name that they've given to themselves. We're all of us Americans, whether we come from Canada, Mexico, Nicaragua, Chile, Argentina. Why should we let our neighbor govern our terminology to its benefit? It can be called the States or the USA, and if we want a shorthand I suggested USam for the country and USer for the people. The conference should therefore have been entitled Canadian Book and Periodical Publishing and the USam Presence. Linquistic imperialism as well as economic and cultural imperialism. A few people thought I was terrific. Most people thought I was a real shit. I'd cribbed the speech from a friend back home. Maureen squeezed my hand when I sat down beside her. She's an editor of a woman's mag called Lady Pluck, aimed at the middle management women, of whom she is a prime example, suited and tied on the job, and on her own after. Her own woman. After the session I invited her for a drink, martinis like in days of yore, in a place that was mostly brown and dark. And we talked. We talked of a regional strategy against central Canada.

And then I said, I said, then I said, shall we go to a movie? And we did, *Letter to Breshnev.* Well, we're a tasty group, well-educated, sympathetic to the plight of the poor, the Kirkby girls. Then I said, I said, supper and a nightcap? Absolutely. So the four of us, yes four of us, Maureen, myself and two women from Kingston who publish the New Monthly or the Last Echo or some other bloody little lit mag, tucked into a small café that served Ecuadorian food and North American liquor. We were very amusing. The young women were such a good audience that

I talked a lot. As did we all. I kept one eye on the present, the ephemeral, the joke the youngest one was telling about cannibalism. And one eye on the eternal, the unchanging, Maureen's sexual attributes, undimmed by these beautiful skinny young things. Her every shift, taking a drink, napkinning, spooning, forking, buttering up, breading. It's a disease, a bloody disease, the sexual appetite, though I continued to defend Canada with ferocious rhetoric. You must not allow your private desires to infect your public life. Who would want to be Antony, all for love or the world well lost? Who'd want that?

Maureen has eyes as black as the Queen of Spades, or do you play Hearts? Going for power or playing it safe. I hand on the King of Spades and two small diamonds. Black eyes like blow darts. Death to the recipient. The lips I won't describe. Why should I torment myself? Bread roll breasts. Etc. Eye glasses the size of coasters. Well, not that large, but certainly a feature, a show, that hides and magnifies the eyes. A body fuller than average in size, for the years have added substance, and in Canada she's a winter woman, a survival shelter, a wilderness kit. A voice like a late night jazz deejay. Still life with Laurendo Almeida. She the lazy tenor sax before and after, breathing a ballad. A mane of black hair. At her age. Goodnight we all said.

Now it's today. We meet for breakfast in a professionally cheerful room, blond wood, tall windows, Mondrian drapes and Mondrian blouses on the waitresses, fluorescent lights, a fountain playing behind the plant screen, ferns dipping into your coffee, and a bright rug that would drive a hangover mad. I put on my dark glasses for breakfast.

A bit cheerful in here, I say.

Have you a hangover? Maureen asks.

I wanta pretend I'm not in this room.

Let me try them.

She reached over and took off my dark glasses. The glare made me squint. She looked like a Mexican gangster's moll. I ordered Alpen, orange juice, tea. She ordered French toast and coffee.

Coffee's bad for you.

Oh, not ours, said the waitress.

Maureen and I grinned at each other.

Can you last another day?

I get so restless.

She made a little shiver with her shoulders to show that restlessness.

How could we ever have been students?

You skipped class a lot, Maureen.

I know. And I feel like it again. I'd like to be a bad girl and play hookey.

The waitress brought the orange juice.

Can I have my glasses back please? I'm dying out here, Egypt.

She smiled and smiles have in the eye of the beholder a way of adding things onto themselves. She peeled off the glasses and smiled, again.

So what session are you going to skip?

I thought maybe....

Hey can we join ya?

And there they were, two young guys – why is everybody else so goddam young? – a promotions editor from Toronto Living – hey, do you know where there's a good restaurant? – ah no, well, lemme think if, uh – so much for Toronto Living – and a publisher of children's fiction from Scarborough, which is even more of Toronto.

Sure, said Maureen. Love to have ya, I said. All of which helps to prove you can't trust anybody, including yourself.

Listen, you know what's just happened? said TL.

What?

Just heard that they, the government, the bloody Conservatives, are at it again.

We heard last night at a party yknow about....

You know how important section C58 of the income tax regulations is?

Yes.

Well, they're gonna repeal it.

That's what those guys said at the party and one of them's an Ontario Arts Council officer.

So, dya know what we gotta do?

Yes. Order your breakfast.

Oh. Bacon and eggs for two. Coffees, toast, juice, the lot, the special, yeah, number four for both of us. Right. Right. Thanks darling. Nice lookin little thing eh?

A bit slender I thought, said Maureen. But a person nonetheless.

Yeah sure. Anyway, where was I?

Saving Canada for advertising.

Yeah, you understand. Right, it's on the table again at the Can-Am free trade talks. Okay?

I thought that was all settled and safe.

So did we, said kids lit, but it's out there again and we all....

We gotta get together and make a motion in support of retaining section C58. Whataya think?

Should be easy. If you think it'll do any good.

Anyway, we have to get onto the agenda and we have to appeal to book publishers and small mags to help the magazines that rely on adverts, right?

Every magazine in the country that fosters capitalism and the market economy, I said.

Well, I suppose, but it is Canadian.

Benjamin, said Maureen, don't get boring.

Okay. What do you want?

Well, we want your support.

You got it.

Sure, said Maureen, already losing interest.

They explained all over again what we already understood. I got caught up in their excitement. Maureen had taken a second cup of coffee and was watching something or other at another table. Maybe a guy who wasn't talking. She wore a cerise blouse, with two buttons undone at the top, as is her fashion, and a long wrap-around skirt of so many colours you couldn't count them, and, if you can believe it, a bow at the back of her long black hair, like the teenagers were wearing out on Bloor. She had quit listening. I listened. I talked. I watched her. I listened, I talked. I watched her. And invented her, sitting right in front of me, and I invented her a future, our future, while I talked. The mind is capable of doing two things at once. What I invented I would be embarrassed to write. I am embarrassed to write. When she rose to leave I smiled at her and hung onto the conversation like a drowning man.

Being with her is like having a hangover and needing a beer. There's all kinds of things going on in the world around you. You're sitting at an outside table waiting for service. All shapes walk by, a bloke in serious blue with a frown that could crack china, a priest in a turtle neck smoking a cigarette, and maybe all the little hands in his lungs are reaching out gratefully for that smoke, desperately, all the filaments, like the miniature mouths that line your throat and stomach waiting for their share of that first beer, rising to meet it more than halfway, or there's a plain woman in a red jacket smiling to herself, a beautiful girl with a handbag on one shoulder, an umbrella and reflective dark glasses. Etc., etc. But your real eye is looking inside at your own needs. The beer arrives. Most of the time you are not hungover and are your own master, daydreaming idly or watching others on the street. But when the fit is on, you are your own hangover. You are nothing else but. You are what you drink. You are what you desire. God, what a fantastic beer, and all the little voices inside you sing at once.

I spent all day at duty, listening, making notes, doodling, sorting out what I'd say to the publishing house back home, a little press, the west and bills due. Mart Kenny and his Western Gentlemen featuring the lovely vocal stylings of the lovely Norma Locke. The talk went on and on. Maureen disappeared sometime in the early afternoon. Our western group had divided the sessions among the six of us and hers was entitled Indigenous Technology. When I dropped in she'd already done a bunk and there was a slide of a sod house on one screen and a diagram of the world's most coaxial cabled country on the other. My session was called The Cowboy Crosses the Border, and the spokesperson, as the program called Leslie Morton, told us that we now even dreamed American, or USam, so pervasive were their images. I dream Maureen much of the time, and she's 100 per cent Canadian content, so I'm patriotic, but she was missing in action all afternoon and for the banquet too. I ate with the Kingston girls and two USer ladies who were nice as pie, mild-mannered as Clark Kent, sweet as young Piper Laurie. We talked and talked and talked. The USers didn't know who Roy Eldridge or Howard Hawks or Jim Thompson were. I'm Canadian so I know.

The banquet was filled to the brim with wine and no one else at the table drank much so I had a hell of a time, forgot about Maureen, and had a dance with a Melony, a Sam (a girl, slender as a straw and very graceful) and a Cindy. Anything to keep the world in the semblance of motion. Jived, we jived, danced with our hands touching, even if we weren't supposed to. The USers knew how to do it and innocuous Cindy from Illinois was a glory on the dance floor. She sprang to life and stayed there.

Is it the wine wakes you up, Cindy?

I hate meetings. I just hate them specially when I haveta be somebody, not myself but somebody who's representing something. Now I can relax.

You can dance like this and you don't know who Roy Eldridge is?

Yep.

Amazing.

It's another one of your Marxist contradictions.

Touché.

You Canadians are so bilingual.

You wake somebody up and they start making fun of you right off. I nipped leftover wine from other tables at the tail end of the evening, said goodby to the girls, as well as I was able. Cindy gave me a kiss.

You're really sweet.

I toddled off to my room. Maureen got off the elevator while I was fumbling with the key.

Hey, let me.

Hey Maureen, where ya been?

Shopping.

Til one o'clock in the morning?

Never you mind. It's open. Can you find your own way to bed?

Sure. Course I can.

Night.

She gave me a kiss, a wet one, a smooch, and was gone. Yeah, well. So was I, gone, too far gone to do anything but collapse into a sleep that took me half way through next day's sessions. I missed one on Intellectual Reciprocity.

This story does not necessarily have an end. I failed to cross the line. Something failed me. It's too complicated to describe. It may be the way I was brought up. It may be terminal intellectualism with complications. It may be cowardice. It may be fidelity. It may be the trembling blue green of the sky, as the poet says, the uncertain hour. I failed to cross the line at that conference. But we were both elected to the steering committee to plan the next conference, on Canadian Book and Periodical Publishing and the Regional Fact. They wanted to call it "and Regionalism" but I made a speech. Another one. I said Regionalism sounded like an ideology, just one more ism in a world dying of isms, like nationalism, liberalism, socialism, and the dread monetarism, but it was not so cohesive a force as that, yet at the same time much more deeply ingrained in Canadians than any set of precepts. It is our geography; it is an economic relationship of long standing; it is indeed our ways of thinking and even our ways of dreaming, ways of defining who we are on the face of the earth. So we should say Regional Fact. Some Ontarians objected but I said that was true to their central regional sense to do that. They were living out their own deep-seated regional imperative. Regional Fact. I can do that stuff. I like winning. I like putting sentences together. Yet when it comes to Maureen I'm tongue-tied. Maureen squeezed my hand when I sat down. She was no mean speaker herself but that's not the point of the story. She was a mean lady carting all that stuff around for years in my eyes. Long live flesh and all it's heir to wherever it's been. If only.

You did it again, she said.

My successful public life.

And your private life?
Well.
Wanta take me to another movie?
What would you like to see?
My Beautiful Laundrette's on.
Okay.

Anything to draw out expectation, nineteen years of foreplay, and the ebbing and the flowing, the long dance, the aroma of the almost, the scent of tomorrow, of possibility, chapter 2, gaining a place in the story, should there be one. Is there an award, like a long distance dance award, for a long invisible courtship?

There are two possible endings, were this story to end. Should one climb into bed with one's neighbour? Because she is almost unbearably attractive, powerful in her grip on things, rich in all matters of the flesh, its accoutrements and flavours, and the very inventor in these our latter days of the engines of desire. Can anyone do more in our sad world, assuming it to be a post-industrial well-to-do world of course, can anyone do more than increase human desire? Ought we not to climb in bed with our wild, exotic, dangerous neighbour, slip across, as the poet says, the world's longest undefended border? Into a world of advertised splendour. Look at any map and you'll see it has already begun, the great prick of Lake Michigan stuffing USam up its Midwest or industrial heartland or whatever. Should we slip next door and inhabit the same bed with our neighbour filled as she is with every lump and declivity going? Should we? Should we not? Have you seen Ansell Adam's photos of the Grand Canyon? Have you seen Cindy dance?

The other ending is the abstemious one. Stay at home but always on edge, trembling. It's an exciting life, no matter which way you look at it. Maureen's coming for supper tomorrow night. Perhaps this time I'll ignore her. Go into the study and work. I'm not hungover all the time. It's one of the steps in the long distance dance. A step in continental negotiations. Face the music and sit this one out.

Interior of a Picture Gallery

When the plane touched down at Heathrow he had felt nothing, except a faint relief to pass through passport control so quickly.

> Your purpose for visiting the UK, sir?
>
> Tourist.
>
> You'll be here for how long?
>
> One month.
>
> Have you an address?

And he gave the address of the hotel in Bayswater. He couldn't place the accent. It was faintly northern, faintly official, very correct and polite. One of the dead languages, he thought. He wheeled his luggage through the dingy arrivals shute at terminal three and the press of people waiting to meet friends and out into the familiar London air. It was grey and muggy and felt like a thin gauze over his face. He climbed onto the Airporter bus and asked to be dropped at Queensway.

You tell me when, sir.

Where the buses stop just before the underground.

You inform me, sir.

East Indian drivers now. Driving into the heart of London. He walked upstairs, as he always had, to the front seats, as he always had, being a tourist, and watched the monotony of London unfold, the endless square houses, as dull as the endless grey sky, brick or stucco, fire regulations from the great fire of London still holding sway. There's a piece of knowledge I'm lumbered with, he thought. Planners must have been military men, suburbs on formal parade. He let the grey-green world wash absently past his eyes. Two girls sat in the seat across from him, marvelling at the new world unfolding as it should.

Look at the green Ford Malibu.

Hope we rent one of those.

Wow, it's like we're gonna climb right up the back of that car.

It's really neat up here.

Hey, is that a pub?

Neat. Wonder what you order? Just a beer?

He thought he might start to remember but saw no point. London. The packed city, the city that hates a vacuum, especially its motorists, but also its builders, planners, pedestrians, trees, clouds. He'd sorted out that definition years ago. Never had made use of it, did not inflict that one on the reading public. It had the decency to die an obscure death. Mute, inglorious thought.

Hey, wow, Shepherd's Bush.

It's real.

I thought Townsend made it up.

Can you get a picture?

The voices of the young, as naive as ever, as ignorant as ever, in need of instruction as ever.

The hotel was three 1850's houses joined together behind a bland facade, and his room was down a long basement corridor, up three steps, right turn, up three more, and it adjoined the noisy street. It had a bed, a dresser, a TV, a chair, no table, an adjoining shower and toilet. He unpacked and went out for a walk, bought a *Time Out* to begin his inventory of pleasure and had an omelette in a cafe across the street. He sat near a young woman he could see in an angled mirror. Not really pretty yet carefully made up. Her gaze was without expression and by the end of his meal her eyes were shut and the coffee only half finished before her. Her breasts rested easily under her sweater. Her fingers were long and delicate. Her lipstick was almost mauve and her lips full, though her face was thin and her cheeks a shade hollow.

He went to plays, films, concerts, galleries. Each day he acquired a remarkable amount of knowledge. He thought of his mind as that Flemish painting, painter unknown, paintings hung three deep round the walls of the tall studio. His mind packed with culture and the possessor anonymous. London a way to pass time now. There was so much to see, so many things to attend, that time passed more easily here than elsewhere. London as spectacle, the least important quality in Aristotle's definition of tragedy. So much spectacle, so little drama. Like scenery. Movie critics who liked scenery. Christ. Now he had arrived by divers ways at the bottom of Aristotle's categories. Spectacle and scenery. Upon the surface of things. To keep from being alive in the present. There was always a danger, especially with theatre, that all the other categories might leap up in your heart and make you face yourself. Yet he piled them in, all those pictures into his room. Invited no one else in. Although it had been crowded enough in its day.

There were things he still liked, almost in spite of himself, like the steamy entrails of Holland Park after a rain, or the prospect at Kenwood. Not many prospects held out that long. He sat on a bench below the Adams house looking down the slope, to the pond and woods. A prospect that relaxed him in spite of himself and no matter what his mood. What is the structure, he wondered, the combination of wood and water, grass and sky, that can act like a mother to a child? A natural world, yet man designed. And lay down and fell asleep.

The voices of the young were everywhere, as enthusiastic, as ignorant, as ever, though as more of them spoke in languages he didn't understand, they were no more annoying than traffic. They did more kissy facey than before, more women browsed on their partners than before, there was more leg, midriff and even backside than before in parks on sunny days. He noticed all that as he would notice a lull in traffic. Traffic remained a mild pleasure, or the beating of it, crossing against a light or through four lanes of traffic. Pleasure in the small victories of daily life in the wen. Cobbett's name for London. Essay written on William Cobbett, what, forty-five years ago? *From Ploughboy to a Seat in Parliament,* a splendid book. One day Cobbett as a young man was going to market, met a carriage of men going the other way to a career at sea, climbed out of one cart into the other and changed his life on the spot. Even found his way to Nova Scotia for a time, fell in love. Life was in those days far more vicissitudinous than it is today, as he had explained to his students in a lecture proving how much more real melodrama had once been. Well, there it was, Cobbett, hung on the wall. In the room no one visited, for all the teaching is dead and gone.

He had appetites. He got hungry and had to eat. As cheaply as possible as always, as if he were still a graduate student. He walked the old streets. Today down the Earl's Court, which he had entirely forgotten. I must have walked it fifty times that first time here, he thought, between the Fulham Road and Notting Hill Gate. Fueled by beer. The walking tired him and he had to rest often, watching TV in his room. He liked sports best, even the test match. He couldn't stand serious life-and-death drama. A wife leaves her famous, rotten husband to regain her own career as a photographer and meets her old schoolfriends who are coping with life in complex and unhappy ways. Who needs it? Who the hell needs that? How much truth can one person stand in his one lifetime?

Once he drank a Saturday night away. He didn't meet anyone, talk to anyone, just stayed in the Prince of Wales till closing time. By then he felt at home because everyone else in the place had come later than he had. That night he was a regular. He made his way home as if in a dream, past the beautiful shops filled with giant vases, blouses made of old doilies, a window full of bowler hats and old school ties, or antique bureaus and oil paintings of flowers, or plain old smelly fish and chips. There is a class distinction in England, those on the last bus with steaming vinegar-laden chips and those without. Karl Marx had never eaten fish and chips so what the hell was all the revolutionary fuss about? Anyway. He didn't walk a straight line, but who did on a London street? He collapsed in bed, woke up with his clothes on and a terrible hangover. He felt a hole in his chest like his guts had been sucked out. He was so fatigued he could hardly manage to take an Aspirin or pour a glass of Perrier water. All day long it was like that. Sometimes it would improve for ten minutes, after he had a beer or a hamburger or another Aspirin. He wondered now when he had a hangover if it would be his last, like this trip to London. That's why he took it, to do it one more time. At least. Consumed with that which we were nourished by. Taught that a hundred times. He went back to the pub at ten.

And how are ya today?

Still alive.

And what would you have, sir?

Pint of lager, with ice cubes in it.

Well dat's a new one.

The blond lager slid down his throat to the desert within that sucked it up like it was the year's first rain. Jesus, that's good, and he had another and went home to bed. As he was about to fall asleep he waved his hangover goodbye like an old friend he might not see again. And fell asleep.

Next morning he felt good. He looked himself all over but he still felt good. The sun was actually shining and he felt the warmth inside himself. I'm old enough to know better, he thought, but went walking again in Kensington Gardens. By the railing of a path in Kensington Gardens. Pound's digs unplaqued. Pound who laid waste all about him and gained a long fame. Pretended to know everything and yet knew nothing of the business of good government. Conciliatory good sense is its own grave. He thought of committees, a hundred and twenty or whatever. The sun kept pouring into his head. Well, let the sun shine, it can't trick me. That trick's the oldest one in the books. He looked again at the latest furniture by which life makes itself so attractive in the sunshine. There's long blonde hair on tanned skin in loose trousers and a citrine blouse longer in the back than front so her breasts seem to hoist it aloft like a flag. Her face is a bit snub but progeny is progeny and she's doing her unlevel best. There's a blonde whose hair cascades in curls onto a man's plain stripped shirt, over white slacks with a frill at the bottom and blue sneakers. She's reading a book, keeping to her self modestly but her face has no modesty at all. There were times in his life when he would have given his life for that face. Love o love.

Now, dark skin walks by in a zebra dress, knit and tight, warm for a day like this, shaped as an H around the neck so her arms declare their health and palpability, their brownness, their ferocious youth. Very painted lips. Every woman her own artist and artwork. A short dark girl whose bright red lipstick matches her silk neckerchief; black sandals echo the burst of black hair, dark blue sweater mediates and the tan of course is everywhere. One more example of the perfect stranger. God what eyes.

He sat for a long time on the bench in contemplation of the flesh and furniture of the new world. His legs had grown stiff. It was time to move. To stand up. To leave this dark green wood and metal bench that rested on the great walk in Kensington Gardens. Time to put down your *Guardian*, your *Times,* your *Independent,* your *Standard,* your pulp novel to kill time with, your musing, your vantage on the ways of the world. And die. It's nothing less. To stand up is nothing less than death. Of course that's true. Nothing's more obvious, more trite. Talked of endlessly in poetry. Walking off. Leaving where you've been. Look back. Someone else is already there. Between the park and his hotel he would die seven times. Each time a true death. Each time a step forward.

For his time in London he had remained as resolutely as he could on the surface of the present and its spectacle, with side trips to the future, terminal five, level six care, the last bench, joining the majority. The past he held at bay. It was there. He knew it was there, like the ocean round this island, but you needn't visit the seaside. It was there like happiness. Remember happiness? No way, man, no way. No way, no way man. Ah, he said, looking in front of him, the cement on the street is grey. The sky is clouded over. A thin rain falls. The umbrellas bloom. It remains very hot. On Queensway he saw the buildings as a mixture of Victorian overblown and 1950s tedium, all stained with foul rain in the days before the clean air act removed London from the black imagination of Charles Dickens. Read all sixteen Dickens novels that year. Echoes everywhere of back then, plays seen or read, that summer at the British Museum, summer of God knows when. No way man, no way, no. I shall buy whatever I want, a book, a baguette, a Japanese kimono, a Miss Havisham doilie dress, alarm clocks, bouquets, root canals and girls. On Queensway alone. Scottish salmon. The world brought to my front door, to my seedy bed and breakfast where the morning's fried eggs swim across the bacon fat, sticking out their little white oars and working so diligently to be loved you will consume them with pity. He continued his inventory, painting the long flat canvas of the present. Having been to so many galleries. But where's it all come from? he asked. Well, Constable. From Wilson, Gainsborough, Ruisdael, Cuyp, Poussin, Claude. That's safe as houses. Remember saying all days are equal, the then as important as the now. Said that for someone else's death. Now is filled with museums, galleries, corpses, the pots and pans of a dead people. When the last memory dies that's a true death. He decided he should visit Highgate Cemetery. Then a girl on the bench next to him talked.

Can you tell me the time please?

Sorry, I don't have a watch. It must be about four.

Do you know Queensway? I have to find, see,

that place.

It's one gate east from here, then straight ahead. Past the second underground station. You can't miss it.

Thank you.

She continued to sit.

You going to stay there then?

Yes. For two weeks.

Where are you from?

Switzerland. I'm from Switzerland. Berne.

You speak English quite well.

Thank you. I studied at Cambridge once for three months.

She had a plain enough face and dress, short hair like a brush cut gone to seed, no makeup, a plain Germanic face. Somebody's daughter. He asked questions. She was visiting London for the second time. Her father was in the States. She liked London. What should she see? He told her. Did she like plays?

Yes. I saw some last time. *The Starlight Express.* Did you see? That was great.

He shrugged. What the hell. No point telling the truth.

Can you tell me some I should see?

He listed six he liked best, told her how she could line up for tickets at the National, about the half-price booth at Leicester Square, how to buy the cheapest seats on Wednesday matinees because theatres often closed the upper circle and seated everyone in the circle or stalls.

Are you a museum goer?

O yes. I like the British Museum, especially the

Egyptian Room.

It's good on the Celts, too.

I'll look.

Upstairs. And the Tate has a new addition, and there are now hundreds of Turners on permanent display.

Who is Turner she asked and he told her, at length. She kept asking questions. He answered in detail. Then she had to go, to meet a friend. Goodbye, she said. Thank you very much. He watched her walk away, a plain enough girl. About to enter London. Asking questions. Unlocking the door to the gallery. He'd answered.

The past swelled up in him. He couldn't stop it. Swept over the island. He'd worked so hard to keep happiness at bay. He knew there was no one in the gallery. He knew that. He always knew that. But now he saw it clearly as if he'd never seen it. No one in the gallery, no one to teach, to talk to. It was all over, no one to teach, the young as plentiful as ever, as ignorant as ever, the young as nice as ever. He was alive now and had no taste for it. He was alive now and could make no use of it.

Acknowledgements

I want to thank Anne Szumigalski, David Carpenter, Elyse St. George and all those who made up the prose group that met at Anne's house on Connaught. They encouraged these stories. And thanks to Bonnie Burnard, one of the good editors.

Some of these stories have been published before:
"Baby Duck, " *Dinosaur Review,* 1986;
"Tiger Lily," *Grain,* 1985;
"Get Your Jive on Highway Five," *dandelion,* 1985, reprinted in *The Old Dance,* Coteau, 1986;
"Dead Soldier," *Sky High,* Coteau, 1989;
"Joni Went to Market," *200% Cracked Wheat.* Coteau, 1992;
"The Girl Next Door," *Stag Line,* Coteau 1995.

Don Kerr is the author of five books of poetry, including *Autodidactic,* his most recent. He has also had more than half-a-dozen of his plays receive professional productions, including *The Smoking Cabaret* and *Talking Back: The Birth of the CCF*. Although his stories have appeared in literary periodicals across Canada, *Love and the Bottle* is his first short fiction collection.

An architectural heritage buff with a reputation for his wit, Don was born in Saskatoon and continues to make his home there. He teaches in both the English and Drama departments at the University of Saskatchewan.